Abou

Elizabeth Greehy is 25 years old. Happily married to Michael, they have two little children, Mark who is three and Sinead who is five months. They live together in Kilbaha, in Co. Clare, a most beautifully scenic spot in the West of Ireland.

Having always harboured a deep yearning to write, she published this novella essentially to fulfil an ambition and also in an effort to become recognised in the literary world.

Sshhh...

A Secret Between Friends is Sacred

...or is it?

by
Elizabeth Greehy

KILBAHA PUBLISHING

This paperback edition 2005

Copyright © 2005 Elizabeth Greehy

All rights reserved. No part of this book may be used or reproduced in any manner whatsoever without the written permission of the Publisher.

This book is a work of fiction. Names, characters, places and incidents are products of the authors' imagination or are used fictitiously. Any resemblance to actual events or locales or persons, living or dead, is entirely coincidental.

Book and Cover design by
Optic Nerve Design Group, Limerick, Ireland
Typeset in Caslon Pro.
Printed in Ireland by TM Printing, Ennis, Co. Clare

ISBN 0-9551018-1-6

Kilbaha Publishing
Kilbaha, County Clare, Ireland

Acknowledgements:

I wish to sincerely thank all my family and friends for encouraging me to publish this, my debut novella. It's a scary thing, putting oneself out there for the first time - open to criticism - constructive and otherwise - as well as, hopefully, some praise. But with the overwhelming emotional support from my husband and my parents, as well as others, I found the courage to do it. Thank you everyone.

The story and characters in this novel are entirely fictional. Although it is set in locations that do exist, the descriptions given of those places are mostly fictional with only some mild basis on reality. Any apparent errors in fact surrounding the locations are due simply to the complete story being the focus of the authors' imagination and any similarities to actual people or situations are entirely coincidental.

Chapter 1

She basked in the moment, reclining amidst the plumped up, eiderdown trappings of five-star, luxury, in the West End's Langhem Hilton Hotel. Taking a lingering sip from the wine glass by her bed, she watched as the attractive, young gentleman fixed his tie and straightened out any visible creases from his dark-navy, three-piece.

"Shame you have to rush off again Damien" she sighed.

He turned to face her – his expression rather more troubled than ecstatic, as images of strained explanations to his boss flitted around his mind.

"I have to get back to work…I'm sorry Lisa… …Anyway, won't your husband be at home by now?"

He proceeded to blow a pitifully empty kiss in her direction - about as insignificant and as futile, as their snatched, random, moments of ecstasy had ever been, and thus he left.

She heaved a further exaggerated sigh and rolled over on the bed.

Damien was a fine young man – ambitious and hard working, pleasant and sociable, however, she was not at all interested in Damien 'the person', any more than he was in her. Instead, she was simply fascinated by the idea of briefly escaping the monotony of her own, listless marriage – what now more resembled a union of convenience, than of love and faith. Damien was a 'past-time', a weakness – though one she was undeniably partial to – to help fill the void between the current tedium in which she found herself, and the, now imminent, step towards a new life, that she was about to take.

A deliberate smile settled on her lips as she mused over her move. Yes, her husband would be at home now – her lacklustre, unresponsive, husband - but today, at thirty-two years and in her prime, Lisa Gray was on the verge of making an entirely fresh start and, for once, she couldn't wait to get home to tell him.

Independently wealthy – due to the resounding successes of her fathers legal firm – she and her family were of the elite, top drawer of Mayfair's glitterati. Her modest, sensitive demeanour was instinctive - and she prided herself in being what one might call a rather 'laissez-faire' socialite, …and not a compulsive-shopping, party-mad, snob, such as some of the other moneyed folk that she reluctantly had to mingle with quite regularly.

Lisa had spent the last seven years of her life, in what anyone would describe as a 'relatively tolerable' type of indeterminate limbo. Living in unquestionable luxury, with an indefinite disposable income, and little other to do with her days than to visit the shops, meet her girlfriends for calypso coffees on Bond Street, and pursue her passion for writing - typing regularly on her laptop computer - she was, however, married to a man that she no longer loved and this riddled her inners with regret; every 'seemingly' happy day, culminating in a rather lonely conclusion.

Her husband, Benjamin, toiled arduously in her fathers firm and was set to become a partner within the next couple of months; a classic workaholic who ceaselessly paid more attention to his court transcripts and his single glass of Remy Martin in the evenings, than he ever did to his wife.

Her affair was despicable - shameful; of that there was little doubt. Nevertheless, she had seen the sordidness of it, however distorted, as a form of silent revenge. She felt, rather strongly, that her husband's sole ambition for sweeping her off her feet, those seven years ago, was merely a further effort to get his size nines well and truly rooted beneath the solid oak desks at her fathers firm. Now that some degree of partnership was a certainty, she was no longer a central figure - and his treatment of her, especially over the past twelve months, truly reflected that disinterest.

Oh he cared for her on some, baseless, level, she was certain of that, but nothing in his life was ever going to take precedence over his work and for Lisa, it was definitely time to move on.

Chapter 2

He barely noticed her presence in the room that afternoon – apart from the sweet-smelling fragrance of Chanel No 5, wafting pleasantly in his general direction.

Sitting in his leather lounge chair by the open, bay window in their apartment, beneath unadulterated rays of streaming afternoon sunlight, Benjamin was absorbedly sifting through a sheaf of papers that lay carefully, in chronological order, on his lap.

She coughed a little, somewhat impatiently, from the doorway.

"Oh Hi Li", he muttered.

"Ben …we have to talk"…

Without so much as glancing in her direction, he replied in his customary, dismissive drawl, "…of course we do my love …I have to…em …meet a client at three so I'll be….em", and his voice trailed off as he became engrossed once again in his paperwork.

"Benjamin Gray, …I said we have to talk and I want us to do it now" she snapped, considerably startled, in fact, by her own sudden abrasiveness.

Ben, who was also somewhat taken aback by her curiously, brash manner, looked up from his papers and then proceeded to cross his legs, drumming the air with one of his shiny black loafers - looking intently at her; at this point, quite interested to hear what was suddenly, clearly so important in his wife's life.

Had she perhaps double booked her hair stylist with her nail appointment? Or had her mother, perchance, been visiting this afternoon? He couldn't think of anything that might be worrying her more than these things would, but then he hadn't really paid much attention to anything she did with her time, over the past few years.

She took a breath and with a rather unexpected burst of confidence…

"I'm leaving you", she uttered fast and furiously.

    Nothing.
    The wad of papers slid off his knees, flitting to the carpet in total disarray; his silence and momentary stillness proving that he had not foreseen this little bombshell - she almost felt a pang of pity for him as he sat there, open jawed and pale.

Approaching him slowly, she knelt to his level and broke the awkward silence "Ben, this hasn't been working for either of us …not for years now. The past twelve months have been especially lonely for me and … I think this is for the best, don't you?"

Recovering his voice, Benjamin cleared his rapidly drying throat, removing his reading glasses and placing them carefully in his shirts' breast pocket… "To be quite honest Lisa, I really thought this was working perfectly well for us. You do what you want, you have plenty of money to spend, I don't interfere in your days…I love you Lisa. I know you mightn't think so but I do"
    Lisa grunted.
    "No -You don't love me Ben, you just think you do. You like having me on your arm, you like having someone there when you need them and most of all, you like who I am, or at least… whose daughter I am – but you don't love me. You don't respect me or have

any interest in me as a person. You have no idea what excites me or entices me or …no idea what I spend my days doing…"

She was getting frustrated as she voiced for the first time, just how inconsiderate a husband he actually was.

"Lisa, we will have to talk about this. Seriously. You can't just leave… Okay, I admit I have been distractedly busy at the moment but that will change… As soon as I get partnership, I will be able to slow down the pace a bit and we can start really doing things together…" his voice trailed off as he watched his wife close her eyes and shake her head - and hence the cold reality of the situation rapidly set in.

"I'm sorry Ben. I've made up my mind. …I'm leaving at the end of week – I'm moving…

…to Dover".

Chapter 3

If news of his 'faultless' marriage collapsing before his very eyes hadn't been enough of a shock for the blind sighted Benjamin, then the further news of her move to Dover had definitely been the clincher. He had exploded on hearing this. It had suddenly become clear to him that he mightn't be able to repair this – that he wouldn't have the time or the inclination to follow her on some silly whimsical trip to bloody Dover – even if it was only a couple of hours away – and had thus ranted on about 'loyalty' and 'love' and 'seven years of marriage being *clearly* irrelevant'. He blustered about the apartment, raving about how moving to Dover was nothing more than a 'silly flight of fancy' and why Dover anyway? How could a 'rich, city girl like her' possibly survive in a boring, old port town?

However, his pretentious tirade of infuriating claptrap faded into background mutterings, as far as Lisa was concerned. If anything, she was more certain than ever, that this was what she wanted to do.

Having eventually assured her husband that she would keep their separation quiet from family, until such time as his partnership deal was in place; a worry that no doubt, was the actual, and quite possibly the solitary, reason for his obvious alarm, he finally left for his client-meeting in quite a tizzy, slamming the door roughly behind him.

Lisa stood alone, somewhat relieved, in the middle of their contemporary, top floor, Mayfair apartment. She adored that apartment and a big part of her would indeed miss its comfort and convenience. Within walking distance from Bond Street station and, indeed, the many Oxford Street Boutiques that she so loved to frequent, it was truly an ideal, and very beautiful living space – towering over Grosvenor Street, in all its red brick glory.

Walking from the front room, she stopped in the modern, art deco kitchen to stroke the deep black, marble-effect, counter top and the shining, ceramic hob, which was barely ever used, and images of her countless, botched dinner parties and girls nights in with Chinese take outs and bottles of wine occupied her mind - and despite the obvious nostalgia, she immediately felt a true, and if truth be told, rather rare, sensation of contentment. Although she had just precipitated the end of her marriage and she was leaving, not just London, but her family and her friends too, she was, however, fully convinced that the proverbial 'yellow-brick road' to Dover was indeed going to be her route to fulfilment and salvation - and this enthused her greatly.

Chapter 4

Although, throughout the past seven years, Lisa had not worked, this was a case of life-circumstance and personal choice, and was most definitely not owing to a lack of qualifications or ability. She was a learned, well-read woman, with marvellous peoples skills. By the age of twenty-two, she had completed her third level education in the University of Surrey, (Roehampton), where she had diligently earned a Degree in English Literature. She adored having studied the classics, but her true love lay in writing. Having always experienced an innate yearning to compose and create, she was forever tapping out her thoughts on computer but, until now, had felt, rather strongly, that she lacked any real inspiration in that area.

She was now more determined than ever, to use this change of lifestyle, and rather dramatic, change of scenery, as a new opportunity for motivation and encouragement with regard to her writing – and this was the foremost reasoning behind her choice of location.

* * * *

After over an hour of travelling, at a snail's pace, through the congested, smoggy, chaos of central London, Lisa finally made it on to the open road of the, busy, but thankfully swift-moving, M25. This glorious May morning, with both the back seats and the boot crammed, virtually to bursting point, with clothes and various other vitals, she was now blissfully cruising along London's Orbital Motorway, light-hearted and carefree.

Having successfully found the correct junction from the M25, she found herself following signs for Canterbury, which would bring her in the direction of Dover.

Earlier that week, her Real Estate Agent had promptly sent her some keys for a delightful little cottage, perched on an incline en route up the Western Heights, overlooking the Western Docks, which she intended to rent - for the time being.

Driving in from the North West, entering Dover by the Harbour and having seen very little of the town itself at this stage, she parked by the Marine Parade and stepped out of the air-conditioned coolness of her car, into the blazing afternoon sunshine.

Although the journey itself had been considerably short, she immediately felt as though she were a million miles away from the smog filled, fast-paced, concrete jungle that she had left behind her that morning.

Filling her lungs with the fresh, sea air, she began to soak up the clarity and purity of her surroundings, when suddenly, shattering the momentary peace, a loud, noisy horn sounded - she opened her eyes and smiled to see one of the many large passenger ferries in the distance; its boxy shape silhouetted against the clear sunny skyline, as it leisurely made its way towards the Eastern Docks.

She hadn't even laid eyes on her cottage yet, but already Dover was beginning to feel … like home.

Chapter 5

Sharon Wilks watched eagerly from her kitchen window, as the attractive brunette walked around outside, in next-doors property. First she explored the small but lush, front lawn, running her hands over the quaint, stonewall, before walking towards the cottage, a suitcase on wheels in tow, and began fervently rooting through her purse.

On pulling out a set of keys, the, clearly rather well off, young lady, pushed open the wooden door and disappeared inside.

Sharon smiled.

Maybe she would now have a friend here at last; finally, on the horizon, a break from the monotony of her days was in sight.

* * * *

A knock fell on the heavy, wooden door and Lisa recoiled slightly. She wasn't expecting any callers quite so soon.

Perhaps it was the landlord calling to welcome her in.

She was just about to cautiously invite her visitor to 'come on in', when the door began to creak open and a friendly, freckled face popped around the corner. A shock of red curls framing her jovial smile, Sharon stepped lightly into the kitchen.

"Hello. I hope you don't mind me popping around quite so quickly, but I thought I'd introduce myself. I'm Sharon from next door … I wanted to welcome you …to the cottage…to Dover"

Lisa beamed.

"That was fast. Hi Sharon. I'm Lisa" she held out her hand and the two women exchanged smiles and a friendly handshake.

"Are you here on a holiday then?" asked Sharon, desperately hoping to hear the opposite. She longed for a long-term neighbour.

"Well, for the time being it is a holiday, but I'm hoping to turn it into a more permanent arrangement" replied Lisa truthfully, as she turned around, scanning the kitchen for the kettle.

"Ah ha! Here it is - will you stay for a cuppa Sharon? I'm gasping"

Sharon smiled in agreement and sat down as Lisa lifted down two earthenware mugs from the press.

"Check the fridge" offered Sharon "John always leaves fresh milk and some other bits for his tenants when they arrive – a sort of welcoming-in gesture".

Lisa flushed – she hadn't even considered milk or a biscuit when she had offered tea – her mind obviously still behind her, lingering somewhere on the motorway. But sure enough, the fridge had been quite generously supplied with bottled milk, some cold, sliced meats, eggs and butter. On the sideboard lay a fresh crusty loaf and a packet of chocolate chip cookies. This old gentleman was clearly a kind-hearted soul.

The two cottages sat side by side, set into the hillside, quaint and settled, like a pair of old spinster sisters, but were quite a stretch from the rest of the town, which, once you drove back to the bottom of the incline, extended inland from the Harbour and continued along three valleys into the beautiful Kent countryside.

The view from the route up to the Western Heights, on which the cottages were situated, was stunning. A sea of trees and shrubbery, dotted with interspersed infusions of orange and purple wildflowers; which then stretched out in all directions, as far as the eye could sea, only stopping by the vast Western Docks, with its long jetties protruding into the ocean like lengthy, skinny fingers. She presumed, seeing as the two cottages were practically identical in appearance, that perhaps John Richards owned and rented both of the old fashioned beauties.

The kettle clicked off.

"So are you renting from Mr Richards – John - as well then?" asked Lisa as she poured the boiling water.

"Yes, John owns both of these - we've been here for two years now" replied Sharon. "…I live with my husband Bryan. He's a painter – says he feels inspired here - we moved here from Reading".

Lisa was delighted to hear of another 'creative, artistic' type who found this place so inspiring. It gave her hope.

"Actually, I'm hoping to do some writing while I'm here…fiction writing…I guess I thought I might be motivated and inspired by the beauty …and I long for the peace…"
"Oh that's wonderful – another creative mind – Bryan will be thrilled" smiled Sharon, if a little weakly…. "And it must be a big change from London city then" she added.

"Yeah that's for certain, …" Lisa paused "is it …well …that obvious that I'm a city girl?"

"Well, …yes… I guess it is quite obvious" began Sharon as she eyed Lisa's manicured nails and designer sandals … "but I actually saw your address on your bag there", said Sharon, pointing to the leather suitcase on the floor, which still had flight tags on the handle from their last foreign holiday – three years previously. "Our last foreign break – to Rome" reflected Lisa as she pulled gently at the old tags "…but that was three years ago…my husbands workaholic tendencies meant that we haven't had the chance to go anywhere since then"

"Oh well my husbands the same – if you count hours upon of hours of faffing about with a paintbrush as being a workaholic" offered Sharon mordantly. She took a sip from the piping hot tea that Lisa had just made – thinking that a cold drink would have actually serviced her dry throat more appropriately in this blistering

13

summer heat – and she wiped her brow a little. "So he isn't joining you here then?" she enquired, cautiously, of Lisa's husband.

Lisa smiled. "No, definitely not… we are separating actually and this feels like the perfect setting for my salvation"

Sharon felt herself inwardly grinning – feeling excited at the prospect of a friend she could take under her wing. "I do hope it works out for you… don't ever be lonely here Lisa. …Bryan spends most of his time locked away in that musty sun-porch of ours… its south facing but manages to get sunlight for most of the day; important for his painting apparently. So if you need company, I'll gladly offer mine"

Although she wasn't looking for one in particular, Lisa did appreciate the possibility of having found a friend almost immediately. Her own girlfriends had been very supportive of her having abandoned her fast-sinking marriage before she ultimately drowned in boredom and unease, but had failed to truly understand her need to leave London altogether. They had, nonetheless, promised faithfully to visit her in Dover - However, she wasn't rushing to distribute her new address for a while yet, at least until she had truly familiarised herself with her new surroundings.

Sharon finished her tea politely and left; making Lisa promise to call round for a cuppa once she was settled. Lisa was relieved; without having been too forceful, Sharon had given her the option to befriend her and her husband; and, at the same time, wasn't smothering her with unwelcome dinner invitations and the like. She moved leisurely to her own kitchen window and watched, through the pretty Tudor-style, sectioned, glass, as the red-haired lady strolled back to her cottage; her bright, beaming smile fading somewhat as she approached the front door.

A man stood there, obviously Bryan, with his spectacles perched high on the bridge of his nose.

He stood back and muttered something to Sharon who just pushed in past him. He glanced up in the direction of Lisa's window, before following his wife indoors.

He appeared troubled, Lisa thought, as though the weight of the world were on his shoulders. Perhaps they were having an off day. Lisa was all too familiar with such off days, only hers had been a regular, almost habitual, occurrence - and she turned away, her heart suddenly, unexpectedly, a little heavy.

Chapter 6

Twenty-four hours and almost as many piles of clothes and cups of coffee later, Lisa felt slightly more established in her new quarters. The cottage was captivatingly beautiful – a far cry from her West End apartment - but nonetheless enchanting, with two spacious bedrooms, a charming sun-porch, a pine fitted kitchen and a sitting room with the most appealing wrought iron fireplace, and carved wooden surround, that she had ever had the pleasure to sit in front of. Of course the weather was so fine that she couldn't possibly have lit a fire, but she relished the thought of warming her toes during the cold winter months to come, in front of a glowing, log filled blaze, in that beautiful hearth.

As she finally began to unpack her laptop computer on the kitchen table, it occurred to her that she had better touch base with London and speak to her parents. The thought of doing this made her shudder – not just so because she would have to lie blatantly about the state of her marriage, but also, because her mother generally brought out the worst in her.

Even so, it had to be done.

She picked up the tiny cordless telephone that sat on the counter-top; one of the many modern frills adorning this old fashioned abode – such as the large flat-screen TV in the sitting room, the spacious multi-nozzle electric shower with sizeable bath, and the broadband antenna, all of which she intended to make good use of - she proceeded to take a deep lungful of air before dialling her mothers' mobile number.

It rang only for a moment before her mothers' crisp, clear voice rattled the other end of the line. "Hello yes?"...

"Mother, its me. How are you?"

"Lisa – where have you been my love? Your father is worried, he didn't hear from you yesterday, your car was gone this morning …and what with Benjamin apparently ranting on to everyone in the office about the condition of your nerves and how you need a holiday – what on earth is going on? We tried your mobile but it was off…"

Lisa sighed loudly and stroked her suddenly aching forehead. Her nerves? Maybe Ben was closer to the truth than he realised; but he was obviously desperate to make it look plausible that a wife would go on an entire summer-long holiday without her husband.

"Sorry mother, my battery died on the way here yesterday. Everything is fine though – and I have absolutely not had any kind of 'mid-life crisis' – I've just gone on a break - on my own, as Ben just doesn't have the time these days. I'm in Dover and thinking of staying down here for most of the summer…and if Ben gets a chance, maybe he will join me".

"But Lisa, my darling, you could have asked me to come with you. I would have jumped at the chance to see good old Dover again. Its years since your father and I visited there…perhaps I could join you? Anyway, in the meantime, you should really be with your husband – especially in your …fragile state … but I'm sure he will get out to you very soon"

Lisa rolled her eyes; her mother clearly, was completely oblivious to any marital split – believing that her daughter was experiencing some class of a nervous breakdown - and that's the way Ben would have it stay, for the time being.

"Mother, Ben doesn't go to the toilet these days without bringing his work with him. It wouldn't be a break for him – he would be eternally on his mobile and that's not what he needs…its not what I need…which, by the way mother, is some peace and quiet so no offence, but I'd rather settle in here on my own first before I have any visitors".

"Well, …Ok love, if that's what you want…" her mother replied in her best 'wounded' voice – wondering if perhaps her daughter was indeed suffering some sort of mid-life crisis… Perhaps it was something to do with their not having any children? She couldn't understand why her daughter was waiting so long to give her a grandchild – and she was positive it wasn't a medical condition – Ben had made that quite clear, - if a little rudely – when she had broached the subject, discreetly, in the back kitchen at a family dinner last year. Of course, …Lisa probably wants children and Ben just isn't ready – that must be it… or is it maybe vice versa?

Lisa promptly ended the call – a well-trained, sixth-sense for knowing exactly how her mothers mind works, suggesting that the 'children' issue was dangerously close to being thrust into the equation, if they continued talking much longer. This kind of unwanted interference was exactly why they didn't see eye to eye – this and the fact that she believed her own mother to be, quite possibly, the most arrogant and pompous lady she had ever known.

Her father, on the other hand, was her absolute hero.

She worshiped him; respected everything he stood for. She loved how hard he worked, and how successful he was, but yet how he always managed to allot quality time for his only little girl – no matter what. She had quite purposefully decided not to ring her father – his familiar and tender tone would immediately have set her off on an emotional roller-coaster and then she would feel obligated to be completely honest with him. But she had made a promise to Ben; one that, as it happens, also suited her at the moment, and one that she intended to keep - for a few months at least.

The only solitary thing about her father, that Lisa failed to understand, was how on earth he managed to stay married to her mother.

As she stood up to replace the cordless on its cradle by the window, she glanced out and happened to see Sharon, plucking long- stemmed, wildflowers from the overgrown, grassy patch at the back of their garden, behind their cottage. She was wearing a flowing summer dress – one that Lisa immediately disliked – and her red hair, gathered loosely in a ponytail. Lisa was about to turn away and begin setting up her writing gear when Sharon looked up and caught her eye. They waved kindly at one another and Lisa watched as Sharon headed back into the house, her eyes rolling to heaven at her husband whose figure could be seen, moving around in the sun-porch at the back of the cottage.

Lisa wondered what he was like – how Sharon managed to amuse herself while he painted, and how they could afford to live like that. Perhaps he was a very successful painter? Lisa didn't move in any real arty circles, so he could have been successful, for all she really knew on the subject.

Later that morning, after finally having set up her computer and her folders, she decided that a stroll around the town would be nice before settling down to 'create'. Anxious to see her new seaside environment, she pulled a light cardigan over her shoulders and in a snug pair of jeans, slipped on a pretty pair of sandals before stepping out into the morning brightness; Its warmth immediately comforting.

She glanced once again over at her neighbouring cottage and decided, impulsively, that perhaps she would ask Sharon to come along. A guided tour would be very useful – at this early stage.

She knocked on the door and waited for a moment. Sharon appeared, as light and as breezy as her sinuous, wispy attire but thankfully not as loud as the brash flowery pattern that adorned it, and she greeted Lisa with a bright smile and outstretched hand.

"Come on in Lisa – how are you settling in?" she enquired.

Lisa smiled - "So far so good, thanks Sharon – actually I'm just heading out for a stroll – to explore this lovely old town – and I wondered did you fancy joining me? If you aren't busy that is…"

"I'd love to".

Sharon grabbed a pullover and was by Lisa's side in an instant. Lisa laughed a little at her neighbours' display of enthusiasm – as though she were literally starved of company - and the two women set off.

Chapter 7

Having strolled leisurely down past the busy Docks, along some of the lengthy and beautifully kept seafront, opposite the vast Harbour, Lisa marvelled at how much of a hive of activity the waterfront was. From what she had been told, and from what they could see of the Docks from the cottages, there was definitely nothing 'sleepy' about the large commercial centre down on the Western Docks, what with the busy marina, the harbours and the Catamaran terminal – or on the opposite side, at the Eastern Docks, which she had only barely glimpsed at in passing - out of which busy ferry companies operated from seven separate ferry berths.

Sharon had been a font of both useful, and some useless, local information, briefing her new friend on a rather sketchy, but colourful description of Dover that she, herself, had picked up over the past couple of years; pointing out spots of possible interest in all directions.

However, by twelve thirty, as pangs of hunger and fatigue began consuming her, Lisa suggested they grab a bite to eat, and so they found a nice pub, inland, off the market square, where they settled down to a hearty bowl of homemade seafood chowder and chunky, fresh brown bread.

"It's going to take longer than I thought to explore this old town", commented Lisa as she sipped, or rather chewed, on spoonfuls of her meaty chowder. "Mm, It's a lovely spot" reflected Sharon thoughtfully, "you know, we could see quite a lot of it today if you were willing – there are walks mapped out for folk – trips up to and around Dover Castle, or the Citadel – that's the old Napoleonic

Fort, very beautiful, or up the stone staircase through the cliffs … that kind of thing…"

Lisa looked at her kindly, though wearily.

"I really appreciate that Sharon, and I am really keen to see those places, but to be honest, I have the whole summer for that. I thought I might get started on some writing this afternoon, after we got back". Sharon's face fell a little, before she had time to conceal it with a smile and an agreeable nod.

"Of course, …you must get started. Sorry, I'm just eager to have someone to do things with. Bryan just doesn't stop painting these days – cooped up for hours on end. I don't see the attraction myself…" she paused "…perhaps he's just no longer attracted to staring at me for hours on end …" she giggled, and Lisa smiled back feebly, wondering if there wasn't a solemn undertone to the way she told that particular joke.

As they continued chatting, some workmen, who were clearly up from the Docks, dressed in shiny, black, waterproofs and luminous working jackets, walked into the pub for some lunch. They sat down at the bar counter and proceeded to order some food.

Lisa watched as the man in the middle, stood up and removed his working jacket – he was about her own age, with his fair hair in a tight crew cut and his strong features both friendly and attractive; she couldn't help glancing up at his deep set, blue eyes, that danced as he talked, and his toned torso that rose and fell beneath a tight fitting t-shirt.

Sharon turned around to see what had suddenly diverted Lisa's attention and smiled.

"They work at the cargo terminal", she stated, noting the uniforms. "…Loading and offloading cargo and the like I imagine…" she turned back and watched as Lisa continued to glance up from behind her large spoon "…and they are probably all married too…" she warned playfully.

Lisa realised that she had been staring and gave an embarrassed laugh. "Sorry Sharon…oh I think maybe I've been out in the sea air too long today… its playing havoc with my hormones" and she began to waft her menu to and fro in front of her face, in an exaggerated attempt at pretending to abate her mounting excitement.

The two women laughed, paid for their food and, somewhat reluctantly, left the pub, and its rather eye-catching punters, behind them.

* * * *

By two thirty that afternoon, Lisa had waved goodbye to Sharon and had nestled down in front of her computer, ready to start letting her imagination take over for the next couple of hours, though this proved more difficult that she thought, as she continued to be pleasantly distracted by images of her attractive, dockland worker.

Chapter 8

The following morning, having spent a couple of hours writing, Lisa - sensitively stirred by Sharon speaking of her husbands disinterest of late and her resulting, acute boredom - had suggested that they head out together again, and perhaps pick up some food for her alarmingly empty presses on the way back. She had brought her car this time, parking it by the seafront, so that they might see rather more of this interesting place today.

"Dover is much busier than people imagine you know… it's the busiest ferry terminal… passenger ferries that is, …in the world… and its cruise liner terminal is one of the busiest in Britain…" Sharon prattled on as she and Lisa strolled once again, down by the ever-hectic Western Docks – which appeared to deal with freight more so than passengers …they watched a large reefer cargo ship gradually approaching the harbour; small trucks and busy forklifts were whirring constantly around them… "The harbours never sleep – they can be as busy in the middle of the night as they would be during the day – it's a twenty four hour service…"

As Sharon had aptly described, the port was indeed very busy. There was a clear and constant hum of activity, of noisy boats-engines, of people chattering, of seagulls circling hungrily above their heads; the whole atmosphere being intensified intermittently by loud fog horns – what was more often than not, a friendly goodbye gesture by departing ships, rather than a warning signal in poor weather - and of course the added racket of all the heavy machinery that trundled around carrying out ongoing repairs and renovations.

As they neared one of the many harbours edges, they stopped

to peer down into the gloomy looking, lapping waters below and both stood silently, lost in thought for a moment.

Lisa looked up and out across the expanse of mini harbours and long, extended jetties that had given the marvellous illusion of unfolding right there in front of their very eyes as they had grown closer to them – the sun was warming her face considerably- and she felt a tingly, happy sensation all over.

"What's that then?" she asked pointing towards an odd, quite flat looking ship, moored up far off in a harbour berth. "It's a Hovercraft – a Catamaran I think", replied Sharon. "…The passenger ferries to Calais that operate from the Eastern Docks, can do the journey in about an hour and a half, I think, but the Catamaran can do it in about 45 minutes…impressive boats aren't they? – if a little peculiar looking"

Lisa nodded, as immediately, wonderful images of nipping across to sunny, cultural Calais some day, shopping and sightseeing, began running through her mind; summer barbeques on the French coast, sampling the delicacies and soaking up the sun – she could almost smell the mingled aromas of smouldering charcoal, lamb and vegetable kebabs and full-bodied, red wine.

She smiled thoughtfully, hungrily, as they turned and ambled slowly farther on down the pier.

"The port is in such a good position when it comes to cross-Channell traffic" continued Sharon. "…It is so close to the Continent. John Richards says that is what made it so vulnerable during the wars – the cliffs were heavily fortified against the threat of invasion…French and German invasion …he also said that in World War 1, it was Dover that homed the team of British warships that travelled these seas to protect our control of the Channel … the Dover Patrol". Lisa was interested as Sharon shared her snippets of knowledge, and she listened with curiosity, while continuing to glance out over the green and black looking ocean …while they walked …and Sharon talked.

"…But nowadays, its location means it's the busiest port in Britain. About 16 million passengers travel through it every year… and that's busy". Nodding towards the large containers on the docks in front of them, she continued, "…And it's ideal for cargo shipments, being so close to the Channels main shipping lanes…"

This was obvious as the Cargo Terminal, which they were now strolling into, was awash with men working busily - as containers from two very large ships were being offloaded. As they were chatting, a forklift carrying some empty palates passed them out and stopped a short distance ahead of them. A fine figure of a man climbed out and began dialling a number on his mobile phone.

Lisa's heart began to race a little as she realised he was the same man who had so pleasantly interrupted her thoughts the previous evening, while she had struggled, with her writing. He caught her eye, held it for a moment and as they strolled past, he gave her an engaging smile, before turning away and continuing his conversation. His accent was different, it wasn't British and although it took her a moment, she quickly recognised it to be Irish.

"You fancy him then…" whispered Sharon as they walked past, observing Lisa's, school-girl-like, reaction to his smile. Lisa laughed at her new friends lack of subtlety, and agreed wholeheartedly. "Yes, I bloody well do" she answered, feeling really quite surprised at her immediate attraction to this man, especially after having only just initiated the split with her husband. Of course at once, her numerous rendez-vous with the charming Damien quickly left that thought seeming rather farcical, and a flush of colour filled her cheeks as she contemplated their many passionate encounters, however, she knew that their affair had been entirely meaningless – and that she had never once felt any sensation with Damien, remotely close to the wave of fluttering and excitement that she was suddenly feeling, on merely having clapped eyes on this man.

Chapter 9

Meanwhile, Bryan Wilks sat in his sun-drenched porch – watching as a young hare flitted around in their overgrown back garden, carefree and happy - and wondered morosely, how had he come to this. His nerves shaken, his mind addled, his hands trembling every time he picked up a paint brush – what once used to deliver delicate brush strokes, producing works of art that people were instantly drawn to, now seemed to offer only angry, uncontrollable lines and intense colours. His didn't like what he had been creating of late; in fact, he just didn't like much of anything in his life recently and some strain of cold depression, he feared, was beginning to set in.

Chapter 10

It was two and a half weeks since she had last seen her mysterious Irishman down by the Cargo Terminal at the Docks, and yet he was still disrupting her thoughts daily. Lisa was sitting in her sun-porch, mindlessly flicking through the pages of a magazine, in the dusky evening light.

Why was she suddenly so taken with this man? Perhaps if they could just get talking to each other, she might realise that he isn't all that she seemed to imagine, and perhaps that might then put an end to this ludicrous, childish crush that was presently, preoccupying her brain.

Sharon had been around that afternoon, offering to prepare some sandwiches and a carafe of fresh coffee the following morning, to enjoy while they sat and relaxed on the pretty wrought iron benches down on the seafront, watching the world – or at least the maritime world - go by.

Lisa had agreed. Although her initial reaction was that it sounded more like something an elderly, retired couple might do to pass away the endless hours of leisure time that stretched out before them, she did quite like the idea of getting down to the harbour and unwinding, and was now actually looking forward to it.

The two women had developed a pleasant and, so far, in such a short space of time, a relatively solid friendship. She enjoyed Sharon's company and was more than happy to go on outings with her. They had already taken a leisurely walking trip to Dover castle, on which Lisa had brought her digital camera and taken many snapshots of the stunning scenery from the cliff-tops on their way up to, and on their arrival at, the beautiful old fortress.

They had also visited the town-centre again together, countless times; stopping at the Dover Museum and visiting the many shops that adorned the quaint old garrison town, with their Tudor style facades and welcoming characters. Of course, apart from being quite clearly steeped in history, time does not stand still in any town, and especially not in the avant-garde, port-town that solely controls the English Channel, and thus the ever-progressive place contained countless modern shops and features too, which they had also visited.

They had sat sipping frothy Cappuccinos from plastic cups, on the flat stone-surround of the attractive water feature in the market square and had struggled together up one the lengthy staircases of the 'Grand Shaft', a triple set of winding steps in a large stone-built cylinder, which literally went up *through* the White Cliffs, …and they had stood there together, looking out into the distance, both truly relishing the striking view of the harbour below.

Sharon was a sociable and forthcoming person, and yet, despite many chats about their lives and even about Lisa's affair, Lisa felt firmly that her new friend was withholding something; something that perhaps she might prefer to share, if she felt she could.

She sighed and put down the magazine.

It was ten o'clock, and still the long summer evening had refused to show signs of ceasing until now – its hue turning only decidedly darker in the past few moments. She lit a cigarette, inhaled slowly and sat back, closing her eyes to the peace, and smelling the tobacco as it encircled her head in a miasma of white smoke.

Her calm, however, was interrupted abruptly, by some muffled shouting that filtered its way in, through the open top window.

She opened her eyes and sat up; the shouting continued.

The sounds were barely audible; words indistinguishable,

however, it was immediately apparent where the strained voices were emanating from - Sharon and Bryan's house – the only other property in any sort of close proximity to hers.

She instantly felt troubled by the sounds.

It was only a row, and all couples quarrelled at some stage or another – in fact, on most counts, it would be the sign of a good, healthy relationship – she and Ben had rarely ever rowed, owing only to the existing communicative barriers they had both built up, but she often wished they had rowed more often, as it was never a wholesome relationship - but this was different – this, she felt, wasn't just a row and for some nagging reason, the same reasons that already concerned her about Sharon and Bryan, she sensed, deeply, that all wasn't well within that marriage.

Having only briefly met Bryan twice in the period that she had been there, she didn't want to be quick to judge, however, on both occasions she definitely perceived something was amiss.

Their initial encounter was during her first week; they had stumbled upon each other on the path up to their cottages. She was returning from a short stroll on her own – he was heading down the path in a hurry. He had smiled, courteously, and welcomed her to Dover but had subsequently made his excuses and continued quickly down the path. He was utterly polite - she had to give him that - but had sensed that he was jumpy and nervous.

The second time was when Lisa had called round to her neighbours, unannounced, to say hello and found both Sharon and Bryan sitting in the kitchen in silence – just staring – as if in the aftermath of a row. Again, on her arrival, he had hastily made an apology, muttering something about his oil paint drying, and then returned to his porch, presumably, to his work – to which Sharon had sniped sarcastically that it was no wonder her husband had rushed off, as his 'girls' had been on their own for at least fifteen minutes now. Lisa soon gathered that his 'girls' were, in fact, his paintings

– and that Sharon was clearly jealous of the time he spent working on them.

After ten minutes or so, the muffled shouts finally subsided, and from the far window of her porch she could see the kitchen light blink off.

Silence.

Lisa sighed.

There was little she could do. She couldn't mention it to Sharon, even if she did believe their marriage was in trouble – apart from it being none of her business, it would also be much too awkward.

Chapter 11

The following morning, she finally gave in to the rays of sunlight that had been streaming in her skylight window since six thirty, as though trying desperately to rouse her from her slumber. They had certainly succeeded in waking her, but it was nigh on eight thirty before she actually conceded defeat, and scrambled onto the wooden floorboards in her bedroom. Looking out her bedroom window, she could see the forever-sleepless Docks. A large, ferryboat was heading away into the distance having obviously just left one of the berths at the Eastern Docks, no doubt full of cars and lorries, all bound for France. She glanced at her watch. By ten-fifteen, they will be driving off that ferry in Calais… 'How lovely' she thought.

The rest of the harbour was a hive of activity as per usual, but she felt distinctly removed from it all, as though it were taking place on a large screen in front of her, up on her peaceful cottage perch on the hillside.

When it was time to meet Sharon, Lisa sat waiting outside the cottages; her bottom nestled into a snug stone hollow on the long-standing front wall. She flushed as she recalled the shouting match the night before.

Shortly, an ashen-faced, Sharon was at her side, apologising for her tardiness. "Sorry Lisa. What with one thing or another, I seem to be running behind in everything this morning".

"We can cancel if you like Sharon", suggested Lisa tenderly, as she watched the tired looking woman, struggle to push the flask of hot coffee and the foil wrapped food into her hold all.

"No, absolutely not Lisa. I'm glad of the chance to get out again this morning".

They strolled down the trail towards the main road. It was a good fifteen-minute walk – but Lisa relished it – the way the seafront grew closer and closer to meet them as they descended the incline, and the sea breeze swept refreshingly through their hair; she felt it truly invigorating.

She glanced at her neighbour. Sharon was weary looking and Lisa guessed that she probably didn't sleep very well the night before and wished she could help.

"Are you okay Sharon? You look tired – did you sleep okay?" she enquired, somewhat cautiously.

"Yes, yes I'm fine… I did toss and turn a bit last night. Don't know why…Hey look at that for a boat", she said pointing towards a magnificent yacht that had pulled into the Marina. It wasn't terribly clear from that distance, but they could tell it was an expensive pleasure boat - and Lisa appreciated the obvious change of subject as they continued on towards the seafront.

* * * *

"I'm starving", began Lisa as she unwrapped her sweet smelling seaside indulgence. "Croissants …and hot too… smothered in jam …mm…you didn't have to go to that trouble Sharon, a few sandwiches would have been fine…but I'm glad you did, these smell marvellous".

Sharon grinned at her friend. She was delighted that she and Lisa had grown close so quickly.

As they were chatting and eating, and taking sips from their hot, strong coffee, Sharon leaned forward to close her holdall from the prying eyes, and beaks, of some nosy blackbirds, that were venturing closer and closer. The hunger, that almost certainly growled in the pits of their tummies, was obviously superseding their cautious natures; providing them with a sense of courage; they were always the last to catch a nibble on the harbour, so long as the greedy gulls flew overhead, keeping an ever-hopeful eye out for crumbs dropped by the workers, tourists and passengers; and of course eager for a helping or two of fish heads from whatever fishermen might have moored up at the marina.

As Sharon was tying the bag shut, and shooing away the cheeky birds, the spaghetti strap on her top slid down, reducing the edge of the flimsy material to down below shoulder level – and revealing, to a horrified Lisa, a large purple and black bruise. It was so large in fact that it wasn't fully exposed and Lisa guessed it continued farther down along her side. Before she could stop herself, Lisa had emitted a traumatized gasp and Sharon turned to see what was the matter.

But the look on Lisa's face said it all, and Sharon instantly realised what had happened. She tugged at the strap on her top and once again concealed the ugly bruise… as if suddenly doing that would, maybe, dispel the fact that Lisa had even seen it.

Which of course it didn't.

Considering the row she had overheard the previous night, and her mild suspicious before now, Lisa immediately decided that Sharon was the victim of domestic abuse at the hands of her obviously fiendish, oddball of a husband – and she then realised why Sharon was forever so eager to get out of the cottage and spend time with Lisa.

Sharon's face flushed crimson and she looked to the ground, embarrassed and ashamed, knowing only too well that Lisa had made the connection.

"Lisa, I…" she paused. She didn't know what to say next.

Lisa said nothing whatsoever, but proceeded to put a comforting arm around her friends shoulders - and the instant she did this, it was as though the compassion that Lisa felt, was bestowed heavily upon a weary Sharon, and shortly thereafter, the tears began to flow.

Chapter 12

Believing at that moment, that Sharon was about to let it all come out in an emotional plea for help, Lisa was utterly amazed when, almost as quickly as she had started to cry, she was wiping away the tears and making some half baked excuse about having slid down the bottom three steps at the back of the cottage, roughly banging her shoulder as she landed.

"I'm so clumsy sometimes", she laughed, pathetically, unconvincingly.

Lisa was absolutely incredulous of this sorry display, but guessed that Sharon just wasn't ready to admit to the disastrous situation, clearly having brewed within her own marriage.

The mood was sombre as they began on the return journey to the cottages. They didn't really speak, what with Sharon appearing humiliated and uncomfortable, and Lisa feeling emotional, and unsure of how to help someone who just didn't seem to want to be helped.

As they neared the cottages, Lisa stopped and took a gentle but deliberate hold of Sharon's hand. She hesitated for a moment as if struggling to find the right words.

"Sharon, I'm…I'm not being presumptuous by saying this, or rude I hope, but …I'm only next door if you ever need me. Please, just come straight over if you do…"

She hoped she hadn't offended Sharon, who clearly had wanted the bruise and the tears to miraculously become somehow forgotten about – but Sharon merely gazed at Lisa for a moment, and squeezed her hand, before heading in to her house.

Chapter 13

That very night was the first time, since Lisa had arrived in Dover almost three weeks previously that she genuinely felt in dire need of a drink. Unsure of whether it was due to the muggy heat of the day, or the gravity of what she had learned that morning on the harbour, or probably a likely combination of them both, but Lisa was determined to down a large gin and tonic, and perhaps even chase it with a few more of the same.

Her mothers grating voice began resonating around her tired brain "…Alcohol only stresses the body you know – it doesn't help ease it…well maybe a false sense of relief – but according to Dr. Gillian …." and so she would continue on, in this manner, lecturing her daughter at length on the phone, while all the while, she would be most likely cradling the handset beneath her chin while she hovered around the mini-bar, helping herself to a, more than generous, rum and coke as she spoke; indeed the absolute queen of hypocrisy, and not one bit ashamed by it.

Seeing as the stretched summer evenings were still abundant, Lisa decided at nine o'clock, to walk the half hour long stroll to the town centre; hoping that the fresh air might perhaps, sweep her mothers drone from her mind – and planned to find a taxi that could bring her home later.

Casting a wary glance at Sharon and Bryans' cottage on her way, she continued down the track, feeling guilty, despite their recent friendship, for feeling like a practical stranger – except, essentially, that's exactly what she was. She felt so bloody powerless.

On entering the same public house that she and Sharon had

visited, quite a lot now, during the daytime, she suddenly felt a bit foolish to be going in on her own, …especially at night, when of course it changed, as pubs do, from being an understated, cheerful, lunch spot, to being the bustling, smoke-filled, nightspot that she now found herself approaching; the sound of noisy, tinny, music, reaching her ears before she had even opened the big heavy door, and the hum of laughter and drunken chat, droning loudly around her as she made her way to the bar counter, where she sat down, a little warily, on a vacant stool.

It occurred to her that she would never have gone out alone at home in London, or at the very least she would have been meeting someone, and all of a sudden she felt a wave of loneliness wash over her, as thoughts of her girlfriends and what they might be doing now, flitted through her mind. However, looking around at the young, laughing faces, and realising that hers should be one of them, she pushed any lonesomeness to one side and composed herself.

A young man in a black polo shirt that had the pubs name… 'The Port-Hole', a clever pun on words, …embroidered across the top right hand corner, came immediately to her service. He smiled and waited patiently as she pretended to mull over her choice, when in fact she knew exactly what she wanted. "I think I'll have a… G&T please, a large one…" she asked of the man who immediately began filling a tall glass with two measures of Gordon's Dry Gin. "Ice and a slice?" he enquired and she nodded back as he dutifully added the ice and a cocktail stick on to which he had skewered a chunky slice of lemon and a sliver of lime.

"I'll get this", offered a vaguely familiar voice from behind her.

Although the voice was only distantly recognizable, the accent immediately registered with her as being Irish and she prayed that when she turned around, she would see the very man she had been incessantly contemplating for almost three weeks now.

Wearing a dark navy t-shirt and a cream pants, her Irish vision was standing directly behind her and was taking out a small, messy bundle of notes and coins from his pocket to pay the young barman.

"Thanks…" she managed, before suddenly realising she was all tongue-tied, …just like she had felt when she went out on her very first date with 16 year old Raymond Brown, an attractive, though stuck up, son of one of her father's clients, about eighteen years previous. That had been an incredibly awkward evening - which had ended in a silent amble home from the cinema and a clumsy, rushed smooch, before having to go inside and retell her nights events - minus the kiss - to two impatient parents – she wasn't sure had she ever since felt quite so awkward, but she was certainly feeling inarticulate now.

He interrupted her thoughts - "I thought seeing as we keep catching sight of each other, I'd better find out your name… for the next time that you're down by the Docks"… he started.

His smile was intoxicating, and she was feeling wonderfully drunk, before ever having taken a sip from her G&T.

"Eh ….Its Lisa…" she began - and to stop herself from staring, hastily took a sip of her drink before smiling back… "And yours?" she asked.

"Conor"… he replied.

"A nice Irish name…for a nice Irish man" she said… and she immediately kicked herself for how utterly ridiculous it had sounded.

He smiled at her.

He was drawn to this mysterious Londoner he had seen strolling on the Docks, and whom he had spotted in the bar before that. He was no doubt attracted to her pretty face, and curvy, womanly form, but there was something more…only he couldn't quite put his finger on it.

Any possibility of quickly disregarding this man once she had spoken to him, went flitting before long, out the nearest window, as by the end of the evening, Lisa realised, having dramatically overcome her speechlessness, that she had been chatting incessantly to him about her life, her soon to be ex-husband and her reasons for moving to Dover.

He had related some of his life story too.

Apparently, a bachelor, once scorned, he had moved to Dover eighteen months previously, to work with his uncle's cargo handling company. Born in Clare, and having spent quite a few years working as a truck driver in Ennis, the Irish Information Age town – or so it had been labelled – where he had briefly found love and ultimately lost it to another man - he finally made the decision to leave Ireland altogether.

He very much enjoyed Dover, …and then quietly admitted to be suddenly enjoying it a heck of a lot more since having met such an alluring lady.

Line or no line, Lisa was smitten.

Chapter 14

Having escorted her home in his four-wheeled drive before heading off to start a night shift at the Cargo Hold, he had chivalrously walked Lisa to her front door and smiled as she fumbled, a little drunkenly, though more so tactfully, through her petite handbag for a set of keys. "Thanks so much for the lift..."she had started, before immediately feeling awkward - and she had thus began the key hunt, as a ploy to catch her breath and decide what to do next. However, she needn't have panicked as her gallant chaperone had already decided on his approach – and planting an unexpected kiss on her cheek, he smiled and stood back from the door.

"I'd better get to work – you've got your keys haven't you?" he enquired.

Still a little shaky, Lisa smiled and held up the small shiny bunch that glinted in the moonlight.

"Great" he continued, "...then ....can we do this again sometime...tomorrow night maybe?"

She was thrilled.

"Yeah, ..." she replied quickly but then slowing her pace so as not to sound too desperate, and so she continued, "... tomorrow night would be fine. I'll look forward to it".

They parted with the arrangement that Conor would pick her up the following evening at eight thirty...and Lisa stood inside the cottage, with her back to the front door, listening to the meaty rumble of his engine as he turned and left. Breathing deeply and mulling over what had just happened, the palpitations in her chest had Lisa feeling like a teenager all over again – and it was downright fantastic.

* * * *

Chapter 15

Sitting on a grassy verge, about three quarters of the way up along Langdon Cliff, directly overlooking Langdon Bay and farther off, the Eastern Docks, Lisa and Sharon were awestruck, by the vastness of the ocean as it panned out, deep, blue-green, in front of them; the horizon line clear and defined in the distance. In fact, it was so fair and cloudless, that the bumpy, somewhat faint, outline of the French coast could just about be made out, across the Dover Straits and the girls wordlessly marvelled at it from the beauty and stillness of their post.

The women had met that morning, while collecting their mail, and despite any slight unease that may have been lurking they had decided to go for a drive together, up along the infamous, chalky white, Cliffs of Dover. The previous days revelations had taken their toll on the two women and the ice now badly needed to be broken between them, - and what better way than to head off together as they had been doing so far.

Lisa also had an ulterior motive for travelling up the cliffs. She was doing some research for her current writing project – a fictional story set in the period of the Second World War. Beneath them, lying, marooned eternally on Langdon Bay, were the weathered and eroded old remains of a shipwreck, 'The Summity', which had been harshly beached after a spate of heavy German bombings, in 1940. The tide was in today, lapping over the stones and sand below them, and thus Lisa hadn't really been able to catch a decent glimpse of the wreck, even from her elevated perch on the cliff, but her curious nature had been sufficiently roused, and so she was determined to return to the Bay with her camera some evening very soon. A leaflet from the Tourist Office had mentioned that 'The Summity' was just one of many ships that were beached on that fateful day (the 25th July 1940) and so it became known in Dover, as Black Wednesday – the term that she was now considering as the title for her 'work in progress'; that currently sat haphazardly in the form of many scribbled notes, on the kitchen table at the cottage.

On the cliff's edge, the obvious discomfort lingered unwelcomingly in the air. After a few further moments, Sharon turned to look at a distracted Lisa, whose mind was working overtime; torn between her new story, her night events with the striking Conor, …and Sharon – poor Sharon - the fate of whose marriage, she felt, might just transpire to be as unlucky as that of 'The Summity' lying forlornly below them – and which was certainly, at present, sitting in waters just as rocky.

Sharon spoke first – breaking the stony silence.

"I saw that you were accompanied home last night – you're cargo man was it?"

Lisa felt her cheeks flush in delight at the mention of her Irish escort and grinned. "It might have been" she replied coyly – delighted at Sharon's obvious effort towards clearing the air.

Turning to her side, propping her head up with her left hand as she idly plucked daisy's with the other, Lisa confessed to her weakness for this young man. "I know I've only just met him, but Sharon, he is just gorgeous. He is friendly and sweet, an absolute gentleman…and he definitely has *not* got a wife hidden away in Ireland somewhere. I wonder if it's just too good to be true – In fact, I think I'm borderline besotted with him".

"Borderline? I'd say you crossed that bloody border the day you clapped eyes on him" joked Sharon, but once again, Lisa thought she detected a sombre undertone. She watched as Sharon turned to the sea again and inhaled deeply before turning back; and with a heavy sigh and almost feigned interest, she continued… "So what happened? How did you meet him last night?"

Lisa immediately recognised the insincerity in Sharon's voice and suddenly wasn't sure whether to continue the conversation or not.

"We just bumped into each other" she replied, a little bluntly and wondered if Sharon was feeling resentful, because of the state of her own marriage – because of what Lisa had stumbled upon the day before. She felt instantly uncomfortable and immediately began to wish she hadn't suggested this drive to Sharon after all.

Sharon looked away again, returning her gaze to the stillness of the ocean and letting the suns rays warm her face before opening her mouth to say something – but Lisa got in there first.

"Sharon, I'm sorry if you are feeling uncomfortable with me today…" she paused, suddenly unsure of what to say next.

"No Lisa…If one of us should be sorry, it's me. I am glad you met your Irish dream man last night. Honestly I am – I've just been distracted by what happened yesterday – and the fact that you must think my marriage is in shambles… which it isn't…"

Lisa immediately interjected. "…Now Sharon, I didn't imply that your marriage was in shambles – maybe I did jump to conclusions a little bit – and I shouldn't have, but I'm concerned and I just wanted you to know you could turn to me if you needed to. I know we haven't known each other very long but…"

It was Sharon's turn to interrupt.

"Look Lisa" she started with a despairing tone in her voice, "…we have some problems – all couples do don't they? We'll work them out… I'm sorry that yesterday happened and I'm sorry that today was awkward… but thanks for …for being concerned…I mean that… Now, lets forget the whole thing …and for goodness sake, spill the beans about your date last night".

Somewhat reluctantly doing as she was told, Lisa retold the nights events, pointing out that she could hardly have called it a date, but was delighted to say that tonight would be just that. As she prattled on, she desperately tried to push Sharon's situation to the back of her mind, as Sharon clearly had so wished, but couldn't help wondering if her seemingly strong friend, wasn't just yet another weak victim, suffering in denial.

* * * *

Chapter 16

It was eight pm – and with make-up applied, hair straightened, legs waxed, perfume lingering and nerves heightening, Lisa was stood staring into the mass of beautiful clothes that hung before her in the wardrobe, like a line up of hopeful contenders at a beauty pageant, each, waiting gingerly to be chosen.

She had no idea what she would be doing this evening, whether they might be dining in one of Dover's finer sea-food restaurants, or visiting some late art exhibition or other in the town centre… But then suddenly, she flopped herself down onto the edge of the bed and sighed.

She realised that this was the same dull frame of mind her husband or her mother would have employed, one that she had learned to tolerate but that had never appealed to her. She truly didn't mind what they spent the evening doing as long as it *absolutely wasn't fussy* …too grandiose was simply tedious - and providing they mutually enjoyed each other's company, …only then would she be happy. She had forever despised pretentious dinner-parties and similar such social gatherings; having to mingle with particularly pompous people and partake in hollow conversations – and had always been much more interested in getting together with her girl friends and relaxing over a few drinks 'down the pub'. She wasn't a West-End party-girl by any means, but did enjoy the simple pleasures in life – like a cool glass of cider in the 'Nags Head', or some creamy coffees, laden with lumps of brown sugar, in 'The Riverside Café'. She knew that dining with Dover's elite, or hob-nobbing with the art lovers wouldn't entice her whatsoever – and she desperately hoped Conor wouldn't try to impress her by suggesting that they might. This was indeed possible; he knew she might prefer the finer things in life because, as they became more acquainted the previous night, she had, rather tentatively, made him aware of her affluent background. She felt it was important that he knew - but at the same time fearing - perhaps somewhat audaciously- that if he 'liked' her, he may possibly feel intimidated by her wealth; threatened by her status, however, he seemed quite relaxed about the whole situation and was, in actuality, more concerned with the lovely Lisa herself, than with the extensive contents of her bank balance.

Still staring pensively at the clothes, she finally decided that Conor was almost certainly like most regular, men of his age, in that, his idea of an enjoyable night out would probably involve downing a few velvety pints of Guinness before, perhaps, continuing the evening in a nightclub or late bar somewhere – which would have suited her just fine.

This in mind, she eventually settled on a relaxed, casual look. Donning a pair of cream, three-quarter length, summer pants and a vest-top, she dressed them up with a beautiful, silver, 'raindrop' pendant that glimmered and shimmered against her sallow skin, and some diamante-effect sandals. She made her way downstairs to the kitchen and sat down, drumming her home-manicured-fingers on the wooden table before then reaching tensely, for that same packet of cigarettes that she had been pilfering from now and again, over the past few weeks.

Striking a match and drawing in a breath, she lit the cigarette – and as it sat, poised and smouldering between her lips, a wave of guilt rippled over her as she remembered her promise to her father some six years previously.

"My girl" he had started ostentatiously as he sat up from his comfy garden seat, "...you are foolish to think that these wont harm you – that you are somehow invincible – you are like any other human in that respect…" then he had taken her arm and kissed her on the cheek before continuing, in a hushed voice "…you are my daughter…you are unique and indispensable to me…so give them up my love – for your weary, concerned father, if not for yourself".

Sitting in dusky evening light, in the flourishing back garden of her parents, far from modest, five-bedroom home in Richmond, she had smiled at her father, inhaled deeply and savoured her 'last' puff, before promising faithfully that she would kick the habit. Indeed she had made a stalwart attempt for a couple of years, until the sourness of her marriage had begun to leave a bitter taste in her mouth and a marked weight on her shoulders, then she had resorted to sneaky puffs out toilet windows; trying to mask the distinctive odour from her husband and her parents and feeling particularly ridiculous at having to 'hide her habits' at almost thirty years of age.

Yet here she was again, at 32, still allowing stress and nerves to weaken her resolve, as she endeavoured to puff away her insecurities at the kitchen table; wondering why she was allowing herself to get so anxious about a simple date – except of course she knew why – and the swarm of butterflies in her tummy continued to flap.

The lights were on in the kitchen across the way.

Shadowy figures moved around inside. They were obscured somewhat by the pleated Venetian-style blinds - but unmistakable nonetheless. That morning, on their return journey from the cliff top, Lisa was almost certain she had spied the corner of, what appeared to be yet another purple bruise, peeping ominously out from underneath the neck-scarf that Sharon was wearing. A nervous shudder had immediately ran down the length of Lisa's spine, yet, having learnt her lesson from the previous 24 hours events, she sensibly decided to keep her concerns to herself.

Instead, she and Sharon had continued chatting.

Apparently, Sharon was heading out to a drama society meeting in the Town Hall that night. Lisa wasn't really surprised to learn that her flamboyant neighbour was an avid drama-lover, and was glad, for Sharon's sake, to hear that there were regular meetings of the Dover Drama Society over the summer months while they decided on their next production. They would then begin rehearsals in early August – ready in time for the Christmas and January shows.

Sharon had begged Lisa to become involved, seeing as she intended to be around for some time; however, it truly wasn't a scene that Lisa could ever see herself becoming mixed up in, and so she had emphatically declined.

She leaned forward on her chair, and watched, through the kitchen window, as their front door opened and Sharon stepped out into the evening light, wrapping a burnt orange shawl around her shoulders - to cover her bruises no doubt - before heading off in their car to town. Lisa grimaced at her choice of colours; but although Sharon's fashion sense was unusual, combining a rustic, fluid style with loud colours and brash patterns, and definitely wasn't to Lisa's taste, it didn't however, take from her friends' unique charm – and she honestly wished she could be of more help to her.

Suddenly, interrupting her solemn reflections, a knock reverberated around the kitchen and Lisa flinched. She leapt from her seat, hurriedly stubbing out the cigarette in the ashtray and practically burning her finger tips in the process; waving her hands around in front of her face to dispel the smoky clouds that trailed her.

Shoving a mint into her mouth, she glanced nervously at the clock.

It was 8:15pm.

He was early.

The knock fell again as she tried to compose herself and so, clearing her throat, she hollered, "I'm coming" as she sidled across the tiled kitchen floor.

She unlocked and pulled back the door. He stood there, an absolute vision of manliness. With one hand casually in his pocket and the other clutching at a bottle of South Australian, white wine, he was really looking very fine in a pair of mustard chinos and a crisp, white, short-sleeved shirt that thoroughly set off his golden brown tan, and accentuated his strong, muscular arms marvellously. He smiled at her, as she stood before him, a little breathless, taken with his intensely attractive appearance.

The musky scent of aftershave lingered faintly in the air around him.

He spoke first.

"You look gorgeous", he said to her in his quiet, Irish accent; and her heart did a summersault.

She invited him in.

"He's done a nice job on these old cottages hasn't he" began Conor, looking around him as they walked into the kitchen. "My uncle knows old Johnny quite well. He's a nice guy".

Lisa smiled. "He's a gentleman", she agreed, as they sat at the table – "though we've only met once"…The day after she had moved into the cottage, on her return from that first trip with Sharon, she had bumped into her friendly old landlord who was on his way to visit her; anxious to ensure was everything to her liking. She had immediately been drawn to his wonderfully amiable features and true, warm 'Grandfather-like' demeanour and was looking forward to meeting him again for longer.

Conor grinned at her and she instantly felt awash with excitement.

"So what will we do this evening then?" she asked, fetching two wine glasses from the cupboard, and desperately trying not to get lost in his deep blue eyes.

She poured the wine.

"What about we go for a walk first…down to the Marina maybe and decide what to do from there", he suggested and she beamed. Taking a savouring sip from the mild, fresh, tasting chardonnay, and looking out over the rim of her glass in acute anticipation of a romantic stroll, she couldn't have thought of anything more perfect to do on this lovely summers evening – or anyone more charming to do it with.

Chapter 17

As they walked down along the incline, the bright orange hue of the sun, danced and flickered on the glass-like sea, as it set to rest lazily behind the Western Docks, and they chatted and strolled leisurely.

Conor explained that his uncle had moved to England in the 1960's. As the harbours had developed and expanded and Dover's port became busier, he had established his own small cargo-handling group and now employed up to 40 full-time handlers – including Conor. They shared the Docks with other handlers of course, but there was plenty of work to go around in the ever-busy terminal. It turned out that Conors' uncle Joe and Lisa's landlord, were not just acquaintances but had truly become firm friends over the years, and would meet without fail, every weekend, in one of the small local haunts in town – she made a mental note to quiz John Richards, the next time she met him, on what he knew about Conor and his family.

They approached the bottom of the incline and began crossing the busy street, walking towards the entrance to the Marina. Conor idly kicked pebbles out of his path, as he sauntered by her side, hands in his pockets; his strong frame enhanced by the setting sunlight; his smile enthralling – Lisa was amazed by how 'right' it felt to be walking by his side - and her head was swimming pleasantly, warmed from both the effect of the wine and the intensity of her exhilaration.

"So you and your husband have just split?" he asked as they crossed the street. "Well… yeah … we've just split – but unofficially we have been living separate lives for years now... I haven't loved Ben for a long time – though it seems he hasn't loved me for a lot longer. He's desperately self-centred. Work means everything to him – ...and I clearly meant very little", she said, suddenly a little melancholic, as she considered how her husband had not phoned even once, since her announcement to move to Dover – neither to persuade her to come home, nor to check on her well being - not that she was really expecting him to. Although he should have been more concerned about their 'deal'. In fact, it was in his best interests to 'keep her sweet' considering that 'officially' her family still knew nothing of her failed marriage. ...And here she was, on a date with another man, on her alleged 'holiday'.

"Actually, its kind of complicated..." she began, as she decided that perhaps being up front with Conor about the peculiar situation was probably the decent thing to do. But he interrupted her, sensing her unease.

"Look Lisa, you don't have to go into anything you don't want to... not now anyway".

She smiled, and although she sensed there was no point in putting off the inevitable, she did, however, do just that ... and they continued on down along the jetties, between rows of moored up pleasure boats, that bobbed gently up and down with the slight movement of the water.

Sitting finally on the edge of the last jetty, with their feet dangling and toes dipping into the cool, dark waters below, they laughed and chatted together. He was great... and as he talked to her about this and that, in his wonderfully alluring Irish accent, all she kept wondering was when he would make a move and kiss her. Before long, however, her thoughts were very pleasantly answered when he leaned in towards her and placed delicately on her lips, a long and lingering kiss.

Every surface on her body tingled.

Chpater 18

They stayed chatting for so long that doing anything else went out of their minds – and as he would have to start his work-shift at 5 am the following morning, Conor was conscientiously going to go home to get an early night. Having strolled back to the cottage together, he had left her with one more 'kiss to remember', before clambering back into his jeep. Clearly he wasn't about to rush things, and she was caught somewhere between being thrilled by his gallant and sensitive nature, and also being desperately disappointed that he hadn't tried to stay. Either way, he was now saluting her from the drivers' window, as he turned his jeep and headed back down the incline.

Her head in the clouds, she ambled in along the front path to the cottage. It was 10:15pm. As it was still quite early, she decided that she would open a further bottle of wine, to indulge in some solitary celebrations, rejoicing in having spent a fabulous evening with a fabulous guy.

The lights were still on next door …and as she passed, she wondered how Sharon had survived her Drama Society meeting – immediately however, her thoughts turned to that second bruise that she had partially glimpsed in the car that afternoon, and she subsequently closed her eyes and shook her head, as if to rid her mind of all impure thoughts – nothing was going to take from her present high.

She fumbled with her keys in the lock – the stillness of the summers evening, being enhanced by the distinct chattering of surrounding crickets and the restful chirruping of the birds, settling down in their nests for the night.

...When suddenly, rudely disrupting natures gentle hum of activity, there a came loud, abrupt bang...

...Followed directly by a blood-curdling yell ...

And suddenly...

...Silence.

Lisa gasped, instantly stumbling and dropping her keys to the ground. Darkness had set in, and in a spontaneous reaction, she pushed herself flat against the door, hiding amidst the shadows in an effort to become invisible. Her back slid slowly down along the rough wooden surface until she was hunching low, scrabbling in the dark obscurity of the front path to find her keys. Her heart was racing, and a covering of goose bumps had appeared along her arms and shoulders.

Her fingers finally fell on the small metal bunch. Grabbing them, she looked all around her before swiftly standing up, and with shaking fingers she pushed the key into the lock and dashed inside.

She was breathing heavily – slamming the door shut and locking it, it took her a moment for her to collect herself.

'That ...was a gunshot... It was definitely a bloody gunshot'...

'But from where...? ...And who...?'

Then it hit her – the unnerving realisation that it must have come from Sharon and Bryans cottage... that a fight must have gone horribly wrong... that perhaps he had ...had killed her.

She was immediately nauseous and a vile vomiting sensation began lingering in her throat.

She fingered through her purse and pulled out her mobile phone, flicking through it for Conors' number. With trembling fingers, she pressed the call button and waited.

After a second or two, it went into an automatic message minder and she was so devastated that she practically flung the petite silver phone, deep into the thick fibres of the 'welcome' mat by her feet.

She tried to think. 'What should I do?'... 'Oh the police...ring the police...idiot...' she thought.

Reaching to the ground to find her phone once again, there suddenly fell a loud thump on the door behind her and Lisa nearly collapsed to her knees in terror; panic pulsing through her veins.

'Oh Jesus ...Now he's after me'...

She whirled around and looked at the door – waiting - trying not to breathe so as her presence might go unnoticed - and a cold sweat coated her brow.

A further thump fell on the door and this time it was followed by a voice...but strangely it was not Bryans.

"Lisa – Lisa I know you're in. You have to help me. I've done something – something stupid".

It was Sharon's flustered voice, whispering frantically through her door.

Chapter 19

Feeling shocked and hesitant, but distinctly relieved, Lisa stood closer to the door.

"Sharon? …Sharon what's going on?" she began.

"Lisa just let me in …I need you".

Coming to her senses, Lisa grappled with the latch and pulled open the door. Sharon stood there; her hair a mess, her arms wrapped across her chest, her face wan and sickly. "Sharon, what's on earths happened?"

Sharon stood inside and Lisa closed the door, latching it again behind them and turning the inside lock also. Sharon uncrossed her arms and, still shaking, she opened her hands, palms up.

They were covered in blood.

"Oh God" gasped Lisa.

"I've shot him Lisa. I've only gone and bloody shot him. He was so angry with me. I thought he was going to kill me and I …I didn't know what I was doing… I was only going to scare him and tell him to leave me alone but then… then… I pulled the trigger and …" she started to weep. Her blood soaked hands went up to her face and Lisa unconsciously pulled them back. Something inside her instantly wanted to wash his fiendish blood from Sharon's shaking hands. She led the trembling woman into the kitchen and pushed her two hands into the sink. Running the tap, they stood silently for a moment or two, watching the diluted blood run from her hands and spiral down the plughole.

"What am I going to do?" asked Sharon after a while.

Dazed, and still very nauseous, Lisa handed her a towel. "We will call the police. They will know what to do", she said, sounding quite a bit more confident than she actually felt, as she helped Sharon rub down her arms and hands.

Sharon stopped rubbing and stared at Lisa incredulously. "What?" she started.

Lisa looked at her in alarm. "Well - What did you expect me to say Sharon? The police will understand. It was an act of self-defence and I will vouch for you. I will tell them that he had been hitting you. You were a woman in distress - in fear of your life. . They will understand".

Sharon was shaking her head. She started walking around the kitchen; pacing back and forth in agitated panic.

"Lisa, I cant. It doesn't look like self-defence because…" she faltered. Her head was still shaking, as though she could barely believe herself, what was after happening.

"Because what Sharon?" Lisa asked.

"Because… …I…I shot him in the back… he had turned away from me… he had weakened when he saw the gun and so I saw my opportunity… okay? I saw the opportunity to get out and I took it. I killed him…I'm a murderer".

Lisa felt her knees start to give and so she reached out for a kitchen chair. Sitting down, she put her head in her hands for a minute.

Sharon began to whimper, like a wounded animal.

Lisa looked up. "Okay Sharon but you still have to call the police and face the consequences. You have no choice. It's all you can do. I will still tell them what you had been going through …and you have the bruises to prove it…they are bound to understand".

Sharon laughed a hollow, insincere laugh. "Oh yes… I can see them understanding… maybe they will even give me a pat on the back and a medal for bravery? I don't think so Lisa. I cannot …will not …tell the police or I will go to jail for murder. Why should I

Lisa? Why the bloody hell should I? I suffered at the hands of that man for long enough. I sure as hell am not going to rot in some cell for him too".

Lisa was stunned. She felt like pinching herself to see if this all wasn't just a silly dream she was having. Her new neighbour and friend had just …just *murdered* her husband and now she was stood, here, in her very kitchen, audaciously declaring how she was going to lie to the police about it.

"Sharon, I see your point but I still don't see what choice you have. You are in shock …you aren't thinking clearly…you have no alternative but to ring the police and let them take care of everything; telling the truth is going to be your only salvation here. Trust me".

Sharon sat down opposite a bewildered Lisa.

"Lisa, I am begging you. I will take care of it. I'll…. I'll hide the body… I'll come up with something. All you will have to do is… pretend I was never here…"

It was Lisa's turn to look incredulous. She stared at her friend in absolute disbelief.

"Sharon, I can't pretend this hasn't happened. You've just killed your husband. For Gods sake woman, snap out of it and ring the police…or else I will".

Lisa got up and marched over to the phone on the wall. She reached up and Sharon jumped forward, standing in front of her.

"Please Lisa. Don't do that…Just leave this to me…I'm sorry I came around at all, only I didn't know what to do. I knew you would have heard the shot. I had to explain. Please Lisa he was a menace…he would have killed me eventually"

Lisa stood still for a moment. She looked into the pleading eyes of her friend and suddenly …she had absolutely no idea what to do.

Sharon began plotting.

"Just leave it to me. I will sort out this mess… All I need you to do is promise me that you wont call the police. That you will forget everything I've told you…I will get rid of his body and tell folk he has left me…I will ring his mother in Reading and explain that he and I were having problems and… and he's walked out on me… or better still that he has disappeared or something… I'll sort everything…. Just promise me Lisa…please just promise me… I couldn't have lived another day in his domestic hell". Sharon was like a woman possessed, clinging on to Lisa's hands as though she would collapse if she happened to let go.

Entirely against her better judgement, and in a panic-driven moment of weakness, Lisa nodded her head. "Fine… I can't believe I'm saying this but fine… do what you want. I don't know how you are going to manage it and I don't want to know. I want no part of this Sharon…do you understand? You must never mention my name in connection with this …this sordid mess"

"Thank you Lisa… Oh thank you".

"Don't bloody thank me Sharon… I'm not doing you a favour by keeping quiet – it's the wrong thing to do…oh just sort this out".

Sharon sat down. Her face was twisted, as though contorted in pain, and her feet were drumming on the ground as she tried to think. "Think…think…what will I do? Christ above, what will I do?"

Lisa sat opposite her.

"Sharon, you can't afford to sit here thinking about it. Where is his body?"…She winced as she asked; suddenly deciding she didn't want an answer to that question… Before Sharon had a chance to reply, Lisa continued, "Look - You have to sort this out and fast… someone else could have heard that gunshot. Someone who was out walking or… oh I don't know but …Sharon you might land yourself in some really hot water by not coming clean now…"

As well as her family's legal background, Lisa's decent

upbringing and her distinct sense of morality meant that surges of guilt were already bubbling up vigorously inside her, ready to boil over. Sensing this, Sharon jumped up from her seat and went to leave.

"Lisa, forget everything. Clear your mind of all that has just happened. I have to go and fix this… just remember. I wasn't here tonight". She, rather peculiarly, kissed Lisa on the cheek and with hands still trembling, she opened the latch on the front door …and suddenly…she was gone.

Chapter 20

For most of that night, sleep didn't come for Lisa, as she lay in her bed, analysing everything that had happened. She repeated the entire nights inconceivable events in her mind, over and over until her head ached and she was still no better for it, or feeling any the less implicated in what was essentially a homicide. No matter how often she considered it being self-defence; no matter how many times she pictured the bruises on Sharon's body, or imagined the abuse she must have had to endure, it still didn't take from the fact that this was nothing short of cold-blooded murder.

His back had been turned, he was walking away from her and she had pulled the trigger.

Was he truly a fiend worth killing to escape from? If he was honestly that bad, why hadn't she left before now? Perhaps that was a song that all domestic abuse victims were sick of hearing sung by people who were only mere spectators to their lives; by people who had no idea what they were going through; perhaps it was really difficult to escape that kind of ill treatment?

Regardless of all that, she was now unquestionably caught up in this mess and whether she liked it or not, it had now gone too far... Sharon had brutally executed her husband – fiend or not, it was a fate he could never have imagined - and Lisa, because she had chosen to stay quiet, was now, without doubt, guilty of aiding and abetting a murderer. 'What would her father think of her now if he knew this'. And with that thought, she trembled uncontrollably and tears fell.

At 02:34am, she had scrambled out from beneath the safe shroud of her quilt and had come slowly downstairs to fetch a glass of water for her parched throat. Standing in the kitchen, veiled by the rooms' gloomy darkness, she glanced across the way at her neighbours' house. The lights were still on in both the kitchen and the sitting room and she could see much movement behind the blinds. 'What was she doing in there? How in Gods name did she plan to move that body on her own?' Lisa shuddered to think what Sharon was up to but yet she remained determined not to go over there. Her involvement was already beyond reproach; she and Sharon had not even been friends for that long, and she was certainly not about to draw herself any deeper into the horribly messy affair.

At 04:30am, a further trip to the kitchen confirmed that Sharon was still very busy across the way.

By 06:45am Lisa finally slept.

But her dreams were greatly troubled.

Chapter 21

At ten am, a knock fell on her front door. She sat up and rubbed her tired eyes. She was exhausted. It took a moment before the sleepy haze in her brain began to lift and suddenly, she remembered, with all too much clarity, the events of the previous night. For a brief minute, she wondered frantically, if it had all been just a very bad dream, but the image of Sharon's blood soaked hands was far too vivid in her mind, to have been fabricated by a wine induced sleep.

The knock fell again and she scrambled out of bed and walked over to the window. Her bedroom window overlooked the front door and as she leaned out into the morning sunshine, she saw Sharon standing there. Expecting her neighbour to be both frenzied and exhausted, Lisa was astounded to see her looking unusually calm. Hearing the movement overhead, Sharon looked up, shielding her eyes and squinting to see Lisa. "Lisa will you let me in? We have to talk".

"I'll say", muttered Lisa crossly as she reeled herself back into the bedroom and throwing a dressing gown around her shoulders, she slowly descended the stairs.

* * * *

As they sat at the kitchen table, sipping from mugs of piping hot coffee, Sharon and Lisa silently agonized over their situation for a few moments.

"I couldn't sleep a wink", said Lisa finally.

"Me neither" answered Sharon in a daze.

They sipped again.

Sharon began …"Lisa, I'm sorry for dragging you into this

mess. I truly am…"

Lisa sighed.

"This is much more than just a mess. It's a frigging disaster. I can't pretend that this isn't really disturbing for me Sharon, …that I'm not absolutely devastated to be dragged into this horrible affair…but I am doing this for you. I know I haven't known you very long, but I'm fond of you and …well…I know that you've suffered and …as mad as it sounds, …and, shit, it really does sound mad but ….I'm prepared to stay quiet".

Sharon hung her head.

"I can't believe I've killed him Lisa. It wasn't planned. I wanted out of the situation yeah…but the gun was only to scare him… to frighten him off. I never really meant to kill him – I was taken over by something…by some force stronger than I was…" a tear glistened in her eyes. She continued …"I sobbed so much last night, …but I was sobbing for me…not for him. How selfish is that? I was sobbing because of what I reduced myself to in order to escape…what I've become".

"Well it was *really* bloody irrational Sharon but…" Lisa couldn't believe she was about to defend her neighbours' incredible actions… "…But you were desperate and obviously in a very emotionally charged situation – you weren't thinking straight".

Sharon smiled weakly.

"I wont implicate you in any of this Lisa. I promise"

Lisa nodded, while thinking to herself that she was already implicated far, far too much in the whole horrific ordeal.

As they continued to drink their coffee and look awkwardly at one another, Lisa wondered should she ask about the body? Although part of her was sort of inhumanely interested to know what Sharon had done and how she had managed it, the sensible side of her brain was reasoning with her, reminding her that the absolute less she knew, the better. So she didn't ask.

She did enquire however, what was Sharon going to do now?

Sharon had stared for a moment into the steamy coffee before answering her question.

"After our coffee, I'm going to ring the police. I'm going to tell them how Bryan and I had rowed last night and that he went for a walk and didn't come home"

Lisa was stunned. This was a blatant, lie – but she thought, that was hardly surprising considering how when Sharon had already gone this far, she was hardly going to come clean. She was going to claim that he had disappeared and in a sense, he had, but it would be hard to imagine how she was going to manage to pull it all off.

Lisa shook her head.
The whole situation was ridiculously surreal – and part of her instantly decided that life back in London didn't seem so bad now after all.

They finished their coffee and Sharon got up to leave. She apologised again before slipping out the front door and walking pensively back to her own house. Lisa exhaled a noisy moan and with her head in her hands, ran her fingers through her hair. Sitting in a moody silence, she jumped when the shrill beep of her mobile phone rattled the peace.

It was a text message. Presuming it was one of the girls from back home, she reached across the table for it and wondered how she might reply to a "how's things in Dover?" text, considering the events of the past 12 hours.

But it wasn't from one of the girls. She saw the name 'Conor' appear on the illuminated screen and her tummy immediately started to flutter. What with everything that had happened since he dropped her home, she had almost forgotten about their wonderful evening. And that kiss…. How could she forget that incredible kiss? She read the text. It was simple and yet wonderfully exciting.

'Cant wait for some more of the same'

The truth was that neither could she, and for a blissful moment, her mind was filled with thoughts of Conor and their next idyllic encounter.

She replied coyly with 'well u'll just have to wait, wont u? ...at least until 2nite'...

...And she pressed 'send'.

Chapter 22

That afternoon, Lisa was sitting at her laptop – staring at a mass of notes that lay sprawled out across the kitchen table in front of her – and although the Second World War was the sole subject of the many scribbled-on scraps of paper, Bryan Wilks was the sole subject of her thoughts. As she pondered over Sharon and her predicament, an engine sounded outside and she looked up startled. She walked out towards the front door and slipped into the sitting room where she gently lifted a corner of the net curtain to see who was outside.

It was a police car and it had pulled in out front, between the two cottages. A tall policewoman stepped out of the car first, followed from the other side by a young man, also in police uniform. They chatted briefly together for a moment, before walking up the path towards Sharon and Bryans' front door. Immediately, a cold sweat broke out once again on Lisa's brow. 'This was it…Sharon had started the ball in motion … the lie was about to begin…'

Her fingers began to tremble; she dropped the curtain and sat on the closest chair. Her breathing was heavy; her heart racing; Lying like this was not her style. What if Sharon had left evidence of what happened? What if she had been careless about the body or…What if the police decided to search the house and found something?

She began to panic and stood up to pace the floor. But as she was pacing, it occurred to her that no matter what they found at Sharon's house, they couldn't tie anything to Lisa because she wasn't actually involved in the crime itself. The only thing criminal about her involvement was that she knew the truth and to prove that, it would be Sharon's word against hers. It was a selfish thought, but although she would hate to see her friend get arrested she did extract some small bit of relief from the thought that she herself mightn't, and her extremely tense body relaxed a little. Selfish or not, she was thinking of number one. The move to Dover had been the beginning of that new trend in her life and having always been the one to 'give in' in the past; forever succumbing to her fathers accepted wisdom and her mothers' regular notions, and always tagging along with her husband to dinners and parties that she honestly despised, she was determined to continue this latest movement towards thinking of herself for a change – except, of course, hiding Sharon's secret for her wasn't a particularly good start.

She wondered what was going on next-door, and prayed that Sharon was managing to avoid getting knotted in the sticky confusion of her own webs of deceit. After a few more minutes, Lisa went back into the kitchen and turned on the kettle to make yet another cup of coffee; solace for her frayed nerves. Through Sharon's kitchen window, where the blinds had been rolled up, she saw two stern faces, partially hidden beneath their black hats, sitting facing Sharon at the kitchen table. Sharon's back was to Lisa, but she could tell from her heaving and quivering shoulders, that she was crying.

Lisa reached for her cigarettes and grunted on seeing only two remaining in the pack. She was going to have to buy more. She had decided yesterday evening, that she might use her new fresh sea air surroundings as an incentive not to pollute herself any longer with nicotine, ...and because Conor didn't smoke ...but now, however, desperate times were calling for desperate measures... and these were very desperate times.

The kettle clicked off and steam filled the air around her, mingling now with the cigarette smoke. She continued to look, as subtly as she could, through her window and into the kitchen scene across the way. They were still talking – Sharon had briefly gotten up from her seat and had returned a few moments later with what looked like a photograph but it was too far away to tell what of. However, she knew that it must be of Bryan… so the police would know who they were looking for.

She walked away – taking another deep drag - she didn't want to watch anymore. She didn't want to know what was happening over there. She felt so sorry for Sharon but she was on her own now. This was her mess.

Moments later, as she reflected on how to move on from this chaos, she heard a knock on her front door. Hesitant, she got up. Walking to the window, she leant forward to peep out. Feeling like one of those nervy, elderly ladies who never opened the door without having a sneaky look through the net curtains first, she, nevertheless, squinted through the white mesh material until she saw the black silhouette of a policeman's uniform.

"Oh Shit" she whispered, perhaps a little too loudly and she retracted quickly. 'What do they want with me? What has Sharon said?' she thought as she rapidly tried to compose herself before walking to the front door and fiddling with the lock. "One minute", she shouted through the thick wood.

As the door went back, she was greeted by the serious but friendly face of a young, impeccably turned out, policeman. "Morning Madam. Constable Williams - from The Kent Police madam. I wonder would you mind letting me in for a moment?"

Lisa smiled at him.

Pulling her shoulder length locks up in a ponytail as she followed the policeman into the kitchen, she began "What can I do for you Constable? I haven't been doing anything untoward – at least not that I know of…" she tried to keep smiling.

"No of course not madam. I'm here regarding your neighbour Bryan Wilks. He didn't come home from a walk yesterday evening and his wife is very concerned"

"God, of course she is…Poor Bryan. I hope he is ok" Lisa felt her cheeks flush as the lies rolled all too cleanly off her tongue. "Perhaps he stopped off in town somewhere and decided to stay?"

The young Constable nodded.

"Perhaps, however his wife seems to think that it would be highly unlikely. He would have let her know – he didn't like her worrying she said". He took out his little notebook and looked up again at Lisa. "Madam, did you see Mr Wilks leave the house yesterday evening?"

Lisa sat down at the kitchen table. "No…no I didn't. I haven't seen Bryan for a couple of days. He spends a lot of time on his own…painting…eh… Is Sharon okay?" she asked nervously. "Not really madam. In fact, she said that you and her were rather friendly. Perhaps it would be a good idea if you called round there and sat with her. She will need a supportive arm at the moment" he suggested with a pleasant smile.

Lisa immediately felt guilt-ridden as she looked up into the helpful face of the nice, police officer. "Yes…yes of course I will. I'll head over there right now" stammered Lisa.

The constable turned to go. "You didn't happen to notice anything strange about his behaviour lately, or whether Mr and Mrs Wilks were having any…marital difficulties?" he asked before leaving. "No… well, to be honest, I did always find Bryan to be a little…quiet…but as for marital problems... Well…I'm really not sure about that".

The Constable nodded and tipped his hat in polite gesture before heading out the front door. He met with his female colleague at the end of the drive and they sat into their car. Lisa saluted them as they started their engine and drove away. She walked across the front lawn to the stile in the wall that separated the two houses. Squeezing through it, she started to rush over to the front door of

Sharon's house. Pounding on the door, she breathed heavily as she waited for Sharon's footsteps to approach and open it. "Shit Sharon, they involved me… they've been over and asked me questions and…. And I am really not feeling too bloody healthy about any of this".

Lisa's frantic behaviour was bothering Sharon. She ushered her friend into the house. "Lisa I'm sorry… but they had to ask you had you seen anything. Now that you've said no, they will continue on with their line of enquiry somewhere else…". Sharon's eyes were still glistening.

After a moment's contemplation, Lisa's shoulders slumped. She walked in slowly past Sharon. "Sorry Sharon. I know this is hard for you too. God, I mean, it must be so much harder for you seeing as you…well… you know…"

Sharon closed the door behind them. "Its all a frigging nightmare Lisa. It's awful for me yes… but I know it's difficult for you too; being dragged into this mess against your will".

Lisa sat down in Sharon's kitchen, instantly feeling peculiar. As Sharon found a packet of cigarettes on the mantle, Lisa, subtly, began looking around her; wondering if this was where it had happened; if she was, in fact, sitting in the middle of a murder site.

Her head was thumping.

Sharon handed her a cigarette and then flipped the lid on a gas lighter, holding the flame out for Lisa. "Didn't think you ever smoked" said Lisa as she leaned forward to the flame. "I don't, these are Bryans" began Sharon "but I sure as hell have a good excuse to start smoking don't I". The two women weakly smiled at each other as they puffed in silence.

Chapter 23

That evening, having been told by the police to remain in the cottage, in case Bryan was to get in touch, Sharon sat, staring absently, into an empty hearth.

Lisa was there too.

It sounded self-centred, but she would sooner have been at home, leaving Sharon to cope alone with her deception and, considering her entirely innocent role in the whole affair, this would have been perfectly acceptable. However, despite her obvious irritation, she was feeling rather sorry for her friend and so she sat here now, flicking through the hundreds of sky channels on the wide screen TV – vaguely watching everything… seeing nothing.

Also, considering the police officer had asked her to be there for Sharon, to comfort and support her, she decided, in order not to cast suspicion on either of them, she would have to been seen to do just that.

The weather had taken a rather unexpected turn for the worse – a dramatic change from the brightly shining sun of that morning - as though it knew somehow, and was mirroring how the two women felt – downright miserable!

As time passed, and a discomfited silence lingered between the women, Lisa realised that a waiting game had now ensued.

They were, quite clearly, not expecting Bryan to miraculously re-appear or, she presumed, for the police to return with any 'real' news.

'So what are we waiting for?' Lisa wondered as she glanced at Sharon's edgy face. 'She seems as though she *is* waiting for something…Perhaps just for this whole ordeal to blow over' – '…but was that likely to happen? …Ever?'

She turned off the television and walked over to the window. Staring out at the rain as it beat heavily against the window pain, running down the glass, fast and furiously, and although the temperatures hadn't really dropped, she instinctively began rubbing her arms and shuddering.

It was about five thirty.

As she stood there, looking into the now sodden front garden, a car pulled up outside. This time, however, it wasn't a police car, but a sizeable black saloon.

A male figure, dressed in a dark suit, stepped out and promptly held a newspaper over his head, to shield himself from the wrath of that heavy summer shower. Darting across the front lawn, his knocks were soon to be heard falling gently, though a little frantically, on account of the weather, on the front door. Sharon jumped up, anxious and tired, and let the gentleman in.

Wiping his shoes on the mat, he held out his hand.

"Mrs Wilks I presume… My name is Inspector Darren White…" Sharon looked at him with eager eyes, completely heedless of his outstretched hand.

"Have you found him? Is he okay?" she asked.

He dropped his hand by his side. His furrowed brow twitched a little, as though he were trying to find the right words for something. He was a middle-aged man, with a solemn face and a receding hairline. Despite having friendly eyes, Lisa became instantly apprehensive of his tense manner. "Mrs Wilks"…he began. "You said your husband had been unhappy lately. That you and he had actually rowed about his depression last night …before he left…do you think that he might have been capable of …"…he hesitated… "…Capable of taking his own life?"

A stony silence descended on the sitting room, with only the strident drumming of the rain getting heavier outside, to fill the uncomfortable void.

After a moment, Sharon found her voice. "I…hate to say this… but yes. Yes I do imagine that he would be capable of taking his own life…to be honest, that's why I called you. I didn't really think that he…" she appeared to struggle with the words. "…That he had had an accident, or lost his way… When I realised this morning, that he hadn't come home, I did fear the worst… I did. Why? …What have you found? … His body?"

Lisa darted a razor sharp look towards Sharon.

Sharon was oblivious.

Inspector White stepped farther into the sitting room. "Mind if I sit down?" he enquired and without waiting for an answer, he had placed himself delicately on the edge of the sofa. He turned the saturated newspaper over and over in his hands for a brief moment, while Sharon and Lisa found seats opposite him.

"I'm afraid we have made a discovery". Lisa's face immediately drained of all colour and her stomach began to churn. 'Had they really found his body? Surely they would know that it was murder and not suicide'… the cold sweat returned once again to her forehead and she looked in astonishment at Sharon's unflinching face.

The Inspector continued. "Up along the cliffs, at a spot not far from where you mentioned your husband liked to walk, my men, just moments ago, located a mobile phone, a wallet and a set of house keys. We believe they belong to your husband. It appears… from where the items were left and from how carefully they were positioned, that …that he may have decided to jump – a considered and deliberate suicide".

Sharon sat silently for a moment, before then pushing her head into her hands and beginning to sob. Her tears were real… and Lisa felt they were even sincere… but she couldn't believe that Sharon had gone to this trouble…that last night she must have travelled up to the cliffs, and planted those items on the cliffs edge. Now the question of the body and where it actually might be, floated around unwelcomingly in her brain.

The Inspector glanced at Lisa and she immediately came to her senses, putting a comforting arm around her neighbours quivering frame. "Good God" she uttered quietly. "I'm so surprised…"

The Inspector stood up from his seat. "I'm sorry Mrs Wilks. I'd like to be able to reassure you but I'm afraid that I cant. Not with the situation that we are now presented with. I have been on to the Maritime Search and Rescue crew who will be conducting an immediate search of the surrounding waters. I will phone a female officer to come and sit with you while the search is ongoing. Are there any family members you would like to contact at this time?

He stood over the two women, towering tall and straight.

Sharon looked up, bleary eyed. "No, not at the moment…well, there is his mother, but maybe I should wait until they have found him… Oh God…Bryan, what have you done?" She buried her face again and more tears fell. Lisa found herself, in a moment of sadistic contemplation, actually admiring Sharon's determined twisting of the truth and unfaltering attempt at concealing her true emotions. However, this misplaced admiration did not make her feel any better about the situation, and Lisa stood up to walk the Inspector to the door.

"Thank you Inspector. There is no need for a police officer. I will wait with her until there is any more news". The Inspector nodded but decided he was going to send someone anyway. As he was walking towards the door, Sharon jumped up from her seat. "No Inspector, I can't wait here while my husband is missing, … maybe even dead. I must go to the Cliffs". Lisa stared at Sharon's determined face. 'Why would she want to do that? For credibility?'

Sharon reached for her coat and pulled it around her shoulders.

"Lisa, will you come with me? ... Please?"

Unsure for a moment of what to say or do, Lisa eventually nodded gingerly and muttered something about 'going home for a raincoat', before heading out past the Inspector. He put out his hand to stop her briefly and he spoke in a tender voice. "Ladies, I honestly think your time would be better served by waiting here. It is a rainy day ... visibility is poor out at sea. This whole thing may take some time. You will know nothing until the Coastguard have been in touch with us..." but Sharon interrupted him. "I'm going Inspector... I have to..." she said abruptly, with a great deal of determination, despite her slightly wavering voice.

Lisa shrugged her shoulders at the Inspector, before continuing out the door.

Chapter 24

When both women were suitably dressed and standing alone in the rain at the top of the White Cliffs, at the spot spoken of by the Inspector, Lisa sized her opportunity. Pulling her hood closer around her face, she leaned towards Sharon.

"Sharon, you don't need to go this far… we don't need to stand here in the rain while they search…or have you forgotten that they wont actually find anything…that we could be standing here for God knows how long ……it wont be dark until ten o clock…"

Sharon thrust her hands deep into her lined pockets. Like Lisa, she was feeling both cold and shivery from the heavy rain, even though a strong warm wind was massaging their faces. She turned to Lisa, raising her voice over the noise of the seas breeze as it bellowed around the lime white cliffs. "I know this all seems a bit mad…Lisa…and sounds daft, but I just have to stand here… to wait like any other concerned wife would do… its important…to look credible".

Lisa groaned. Drops of rain clung to the edge of her hood and then fell, running coldly down around her ears. It was six thirty. They were stood about ten metres back from the cliffs edge on the Eastern side of Dover, high above the Eastern Docks, when, suddenly, over the noise of the sea wind and the summer rain, a distinct whirring and the loud rumble of a motor could be heard. Coming round from the far side of the cliffs, slightly obscured by the heavy mist that lingered over the ocean, was a large red and white helicopter.

A splendid looking machine, it whirred in one spot over the sea in front them, the force of its huge rotors sending waves of water undulating out in all directions beneath it, before heading around in a large circle. Sharon stepped away from Lisa, closer towards the cliffs edge and watched, mesmerised.

A voice from behind made Lisa turn around in a hurry. It was that Inspector White again, walking towards her, this time with a large overcoat on. "Seems a bit ridiculous to be donning such a large coat after the wonderful sunshine we've been having…" he began in an odd attempt at being light hearted, as he struggled through the long grass and finally stood beside her. She nodded politely and he immediately felt awkward. He glanced past her at the helicopter. "It's a mighty contraption that…" he said of the helicopter. A further man had also joined them. He was a member of the Coastguard and stood next to them, wrapped up in large waterproofs and clutching what appeared to be a big walkie-talkie or two-way radio. He motioned toward the helicopter, as if following on from what the Inspector had said. "That's the 'Sea-King 61 Nautical'" he started. "…A beast of a helicopter. It has 4 crewmen on it and it has an infrared camera to detect people …or bodies …in the water…" he turned to Lisa… "…So if you're friend is in there, we will have a better chance of finding him".

Lisa flushed and once again, guilt surged from within her, manifesting itself in the form of a palpitating chest and very sweaty palms.

"Is that his wife then?" asked the second gentleman. "Yes it is" Lisa replied glancing over at Sharon.

Inspector White left the two and walked towards Sharon. On approaching her, he placed a hand delicately on her shoulder; she jumped around nervously. "Sorry Mrs Wilks, …Sharon…I didn't mean to startle you. I just wanted to suggest that perhaps you should be at home. There's no good in you upsetting yourself even more out here".

Sharon shook her head and continued to stare silently out at the ocean.

Inspector White sighed and returned to Lisa and the other gentleman. "Ron, I'm going to head back to town. I've been called out on another job so, if there is any news, ring me".

Ron nodded. "Sure, no problem Mr White"

With that, a tired looking Inspector White gestured a goodbye to Lisa and plodded his way through the billowy wet grass, back to wherever his car was parked. Lisa turned to 'Ron'.

"If he did jump in, …what would the chances of finding him actually be?" she stammered, interested to find out how long they might stay searching. "Well", he began, "An awful lot would honestly depend on the timescale. If he delayed a lot before … well… before he did it, then there might be a reasonable chance that he is still in the vicinity. On the other hand, if he jumped immediately after he got here last night, then …what with current and strong tides, …", he left the sentence hang in mid air. Lisa turned back to the sea and to Sharon's rigid form ahead of them, standing silently in the mist and rain.

Looking from one troubled woman back to another, Ron cleared his throat. "Like I said, if he is still there, the infra red will pick him up".

As Lisa attempted to take this in, her phone started to ring and vibrate in her pocket. Having intended to knock it on silent earlier that afternoon, she groaned now at its timing. All she needed now was a nagging call from her mother, just to ensure her mood stayed well and truly despondent. Pulling the phone from inside her coat, shielding it from the heavy drops, she realised that once again, Conors name was flashing across its screen.

Excusing herself to Ron, she held the phone to her ear and began to walk back towards the roadside. "Hi" she said, practically having to shout over the rain.

Conors crisp voice sent a tremble through her body as he asked her where she was. "...You sound like you're outside..." he enquired.

"It's a long story. I'm up on the Cliffs...My neighbours husband has gone missing since last night. They think that he might have jumped". Conor whistled.

"Shit that's serious... are you okay? How is your neighbour? Sharon isn't it?"

Lisa glanced back at Sharon who hadn't moved an inch, still staring at the helicopter as it circled around the waters in front of her. Joining it now, in its futile search, was the Dover Lifeboat, jigging up and down rather roughly on the lapping waters.

"She's shell-shocked," replied Lisa, truthfully. "God Conor, this is so awful. I feel just... helpless... and..." Conor interjected. "Whereabouts are you. I'm coming up".

Chapter 25

It was nearing 8:00pm. Dusk was well and truly settling, the rain had only slightly let up and visibility was now poorer than ever. With Conor stood by her side, Lisa felt even guiltier, than she had before, as they continued to watch the helicopter and lifeboat moving farther off out to sea. Sharon walked back to them, her hands shivering, her face wet from a mixture of raindrops and cool sea spray.

Lisa held out her arm. "Sharon you're frozen. Come on, please…lets get out of here…"

Sharon nodded. She looked up at Conor, her first acknowledgement of his presence there on the cliffs.

He offered his arm to support Sharon as she struggled over some of the soggy, deep grass. "I'm so sorry about your husband…" he began. Sharon nodded weakly. "Thanks… I don't suppose they'll find him now…"

Conor didn't reply.

* * * *

Back at Lisa's cottage, Conor started to light a small fire in that big hearth in the front room. Before long, a warm blaze was glowing brightly and Sharon was sat in front of it, clutching tightly at a hot mug of coffee.

Lisa strolled over and poured a sizeable drop of whiskey into Sharon's coffee and then proceeded to do the same to both hers and Conors. "God knows we need it tonight" she said. Conor sipped and squinted. "Are you sure you put in enough?" he asked sarcastically and Lisa grinned. "It'll put hairs on your chest" she offered lightly.

Sharon sipped hers, but remained quiet.

A discomfited silence fell.

After a moment or two, Lisa spoke. "Look, Sharon, if you want to stay here tonight, you're more than welcome" she suggested quietly.

Looking from Lisa to Conor, Sharon felt distinctly like it would be a 'threes a crowd' situation, so she shook her head. "Thanks Lisa, but I'd sooner be at home…."she hesitated and looked at Conor. "…In case they find him before nightfall" she finished, cautiously.

Lisa sighed. She hated the lies. Already, she was lying to Conor. And this wasn't any ordinary, petty, white lie – this was a huge, horrendous, life and death type of lie. How did she manage to get herself caught up in this mess?

Conor got up to leave… "No Sharon, don't go home on my account. You should be here with Lisa…you should have a friend at a time like this"

Anxious for him to stay, Lisa threw a desperate glance at Sharon, pleading at her with her eyes. Sharon saw the anticipation in Lisa's face and immediately stood up.

"I won't hear of it Conor. It was nice to meet you… pity it had to be in such…dire circumstances". Without another word, Sharon put back on her coat and headed for the door.

It shut loudly behind her.

Still standing, ready to leave, with his hands in his back pockets and a perplexed look on his face, Conor looked around at Lisa. Her face was drawn and tired but, as far as he was concerned, she looked as gorgeous as ever. "You must be wrecked", he said as he stood there, looking enticingly good; dressed in close-fitting, lengthy, stone -washed jeans - and with his fitted black shirt, open at the top, hinting alluringly at his tanned chest. She thought how fashionable he was, for a man who worked on the Docks all day long and then realised how stereotypical a thought that had been.

Lisa got up and walked across the room. Standing opposite him, locking the entire days events at the farthermost corner of her mind for the time being, she smiled and whispered boldly "not as tired as you might think".

Chapter 26

When Lisa rolled over in her bed the following morning, delicately covered by wrinkled, lilac sheets she was greeted by a strong, muscular torso.

Conor, propped up on one arm, was gazing affectionately at her.

"My morning face, isn't my best face" she said defensively and she blushed, self-consciously under his stare.

It was quite some time since Ben had gazed at her that way – if ever, and Damien? Well, they just been a pastime for each other – he rarely ever had longer than his bare lunch-hour to spend frolicking, never mind time to waste 'gazing' at puffy eyes and laughter lines.

"Your face is lovely any time" Conor replied with a grin.

"Oh for Gods sake, …get me a sick-bag" she joked, amused by his starry-eyed nonsense.

Her night with Conor had been magical and for almost the entire time, she had managed to forget her ordeal. Now, however, with early mornings' sweet-smelling, clarity, came the overpowering stench of reality; and regardless of the gorgeous specimen that now lay, scantily clad alongside her in her bed, she began to feel a distinct anti-climax.

Conor immediately noticed the change, as Lisa's face became anxious. She sat up in the bed, clinging tightly to the sheet around her. "What's wrong?" he asked, concerned. "Is it Sharon?"

"…Yeah, I guess… I wonder how she is…if she managed to sleep, even a little bit, last night…I'd better get round there"

"Mmm …Its tough on her alright", he said thoughtfully as

Lisa scrambled out of bed.

Conor looked at his watch. It was seven thirty. Mornings' glow illuminated the room through the small skylight on the slanting roof. Tugging her dressing gown around her shoulders, Lisa padded barefoot across the wooden floor to the window and pulled back the curtains to look out.

The Docks, in the distance, lay veiled under a light mist. However, the rain had stopped and a watery sun was desperately trying to poke its way through the clouds. "Today will be nicer I think" began Lisa, thinking of the mild summer storm they had experienced the day before.

Conor had begun getting dressed behind her.

"That will make the search a bit easier for the Coastguard" he noted, as he tied up the laces on his boots.

Lisa hung her head. They were searching for nothing. Searching on the mere whim of a deranged wife – who was deceiving them in a desperate attempt at trying to cover her tracks. The amount of money, time, energy and concern, that was being wasted by this pointless hunt for Bryan Wilks' body, was really bothering her.

"Do you think they are out there already?" she asked.

"I'd say so. They would have re-started the search at dawn – as soon as there was enough light to work with".

Conor now stood by her side at the window. "Nice view…" he started.

"Yeah, its lovely" she said staring far off into the moody ocean.

Putting his arms around her waist, he continued tenderly …"I meant …the view in here".

Immediately, she felt herself melt.

* * * *

Following a mug of tea and some rushed toast, Conor was gone; He was due to meet his uncle in the town centre that morning. Lisa was daydreaming about the new 'love of her life', when she was jolted out of dreamland, to the whiff of burning bacon, and by the sound of Sharon's distressed voice in the distance. Rushing first to turn off the grill, and scraping the spoilt meat into the bin, she then opened the front door, and cautiously looked out.

Sharon was stooped over in the lawn, sobbing. Their friendly-faced old landlord was there; arm around her shoulder, a look of horror on his face. Lisa sighed.

And so the lie continued…

She walked over to the pair. "Hello John" she started. He looked at her, with watery eyes. "A lovely man was Bryan. I'm stunned. … Really I can't believe this horrible news". Lisa nodded in solemn agreement.

"Sharon, are you okay?" she asked, rubbing her arm gently. Sharon looked up. She was snivelling and sniffing and looked like she had been crying all night long. Lisa watched as she wiped her eyes with a tissue; convincing, like a well versed actress. "Thanks Lisa. I'm okay…considering".

'*Mmm, considering you've shot your husband, hidden the body and invented his suicide*' thought Lisa to herself. She was beginning to get riled by all the feigned grief… and intended to say it to Sharon as soon as they were on their own.

"Anything you need…anything at all, you just let me know", offered the generous old man before turning away, grief stricken and shocked, and heading back to his car on the roadside.

The two women went inside Lisa's house, and from her pants pocket, Sharon produced some cigarettes. They smoked in silence for a while, amidst the pungent combined aromas of tobacco, coffee and burnt bacon.

All Lisa wanted to do was selfishly revel in the delight of her new man, her new home and her newfound lust for life – but a large damp cloud had descended on all of that in the past 36 hours – and she wasn't referring to the weather.

"I'm amazed at how good you are at lying", she said eventually, breaking the cold silence with a distinctly cross tone.

Sharon appeared instantly hurt. "Lisa, I'm not finding this easy you know"

"Well it looks that way Sharon. I know it's not *easy* for you …at least it shouldn't be anyway, but …well…I'm having trouble watching you 'grieve'. I mean…you killed him! And yet you seem to be …genuinely crying for him…it just doesn't seem right"

Sharon immediately retorted, "Lisa, just because I pulled the trigger, it doesn't mean that I'm not grieving. If anything, I'm grieving more than most… grief and guilt, all knotted into one. I haven't stopped crying since yesterday. I …I feel so bad…" she dragged deeply on her cigarette and exhaled slowly; watching the smoke swirl around her face before continuing gradually, her face distant as though suddenly immersed in memories. "…We were married for nine years. In fact, this September, we'd be celebrating our tenth anniversary. I did love him you know… enough to hide his bruises and sweep his abuse under the carpet for so long… To be honest, I think I loved him even more than I realised".

Tears returned once again to her tired eyes. "The night it happened, I seemed to be running on adrenalin. I stayed up all night…. Concocting my story - I even drove to the cliffs to plant his stuff by the cliffs edge. I wasn't sorry that night…sobbing non stop…but not sorry…not even the following morning…just flustered…panicked. But then yesterday…watching them search the waters… I began to almost believe that he was in there… that he *had* jumped…I truly began to…well…grieve"

In a distorted sort of way, it made sense. Lisa understood that despite the abuse, he was still her husband and she had to have loved him once upon a time. Heck, she had even loved Ben once upon a time. And if he died tomorrow, she would quite genuinely grieve for him… but then…he had never hit her… He was a selfish bastard that's for sure, but avarice alone wasn't a crime – it was what you did with it that mattered.

Yes, …she would definitely grieve.

Feeling as though she understood now, even just a little bit better, she gave Sharon a small but reassuring grin to soften the mood. Sharon smiled back, through her tears.

Chapter 27

The light mist, which had lingered lazily until late in the morning, had finally left… So had Sharon.

However, the sun never truly managed to break its way through the clouds, like Lisa had hoped, and thus the day remained dull and gloomy, with a constant threat of rain. Lisa had spent the afternoon alone, writing; trying desperately to take her mind off the ongoing search; off the dead man whose murder she was helping to conceal; off their teacher at the private Catholic school she had attended, whose regular chanting of 'The Commandments' and 'good Christian living', now recurred hauntingly in her brain. Staring pensively at her computer screen she felt that if she lost herself within the fictional confines of her novel for a few hours, she might just be able to briefly escape the overwhelming guilt, which continued to bubble around in the pit of her belly.

Having tried that, in vain, for little over an hour, she then decided to try scrubbing away some of the 'shame', by soaking herself in a steaming hot bubble bath, for so long that her fingers and toes wrinkled like a prune. When she stepped out, dripping mini-mounds of fluffy lavender suds on the bathroom floor, she was physically glowing - but emotionally, …remained as black as ever.

Finally, still unable to relax, she had walked across to Sharon's.

It was nine thirty that evening before Inspector White had arrived, somewhat crestfallen, at the door, the bearer of no real news – which had actually brought a distinct relief to the two women.

When he stepped inside, his face was drawn and pale. He was tired and really had little to report. "They've spent the entire day searching Sharon" he started. She shook her head and closed her eyes. He continued. "They expanded their boundaries, following the tide and currents right around the cliffs …but they got nothing – not the slightest thing. …I'm very sorry Sharon"

She sighed. "Will they keep searching tomorrow?"

He looked from Sharon to Lisa and then back to Sharon, as if wondering should he go on. Sharon answered the look on his face. "You can talk to me in front of Lisa… She's been a great ease to me".

Satisfied, The Inspector continued. His voice was gentle and sensitive but his words were very clear. "It's not looking good. … Those tides are viscous. Yes they will continue searching but I think perhaps you should take it, at this stage, that your husband's body might not be recovered. There is a chance that if the body has already dropped, it may resurface again soon, due to expanding gasses and that …so the team will remain active for some time. Also my officers are still conducting their on-land enquiries but so far they too have turned up nothing".

"On land enquiries? What do you mean?" asked Sharon nervously.

"Standard procedure… Just enquiring in the vicinity…whether folk had seen him before he disappeared, if he had spoken to anyone recently about any new plans or displayed any odd behaviour". He sighed. "Look, his credit cards were in his wallet, along with some cash – and you've been able to produce his passport. Without those or his mobile phone, and considering where they were found, it does appear that suicide is the most likely explanation…unless…" he paused.

"Unless what?" asked Sharon.

"…Unless …that's what he wanted us to think".

"What do you mean", snapped Sharon defensively – almost too defensively.

"Like I said…" he began "…suicide is the likeliest explanation, but if he really wanted to disappear without trace, he could, with enough homework, have set up the whole thing as a ploy…I know its harsh Sharon, but it is a possibility" he lowered his voice, glancing again at Lisa as though feeling awkward "…you did mention he was in some debt" he continued quietly.

Sharon flushed. She hadn't mentioned that aspect to Lisa.

She shook her head again and argued, "But his state of mind… he was depressed…he would have had to put too much calculation – too much thought into that kind of an operation … Anyway he wouldn't want to start again …not without me…He wouldn't have left me like that…" stammered Sharon.

"Well, I hate to be blunt Sharon, but the alternative still indicates that he left you… in fact, in probably the cruellest way possible".

Sharon nodded reluctantly… "…Okay true enough - But he obviously felt he had no way out… he was clearly messed up… Inspector, I might never forgive him for it but at least I can understand it".

"Yes, yes of course… I didn't mean to sound insensitive… Look Sharon, without a body at this stage, we cannot exactly 'close the book' on it…so as to speak. However, I think you can accept that we will most likely be drawing the conclusion of suicide…"

Such blunt and blatant honesty would have been, in a normal situation, very difficult to hear. However, for Sharon and Lisa, it merely meant that as long as they believed he took his own life, their shared sordid secret was safe… for the time being at least.

And a strange sense of relief washed over the women as the Inspector finally tipped his brown tweed cap at them and drove off.

They weren't out of the woods yet, but Sharon was praying it wouldn't be long.

"I hope they don't spend too much time pursuing that notion of him setting it all up", said Lisa anxiously; afraid that more enquiries might eventually lead the police back to Sharon, and subsequently, back to Lisa.

"They won't. I'm sure of it", replied Sharon – though her wavering voice didn't bear out her wishful confidence.

Lisa walked across to Sharon's drinks cabinet and lifted down a bottle of vodka that sat on the top shelf. "Do you mind?" she asked, with a needy tone in her voice. Sharon agreed that alcohol was, without question, required to settle their nerves and so she fetched two tall, slim glasses from the kitchen cupboard.

As they sipped on the vodka, which Sharon lightly diluted with soda water, Lisa kept glancing at her mobile phone. Sharon guessed she was expecting a call from Conor.

"So he stayed last night then?" asked Sharon. She wasn't completely certain about this flighty Irishman, but was desperate to change the subject to something she was sure would bring a smile to Lisa's face. She was right. The mere mention of his name brought a rosy hue to her wan cheeks. "Yes he stayed" she replied.

"Come on then, fill me in" coaxed Sharon playfully.

Lisa smiled. "I don't kiss and tell Sharon, but let me just say that I was most definitely looking for an encore"

* * * *

The following morning, Lisa's stomach churned from the vodka – and her mouth felt as dry as the Gobi in a heat wave. As the evening before had progressed, and the two women had chatted about their lives, the soda water had eventually run dry, the shots of vodka subsequently became neat and cigarettes were smoked in abundance; until only empty glasses, two crumpled cardboard boxes, and an over flowing ash tray remained.

Although they had discussed many things at length, including love and friendship, they had widely avoided the subject of Bryan's body. Lisa did not want to make a 'drunken faux pas' by asking Sharon where it was, and then have that grisly image haunting her for evermore.

Also, it was an ease to talk of something other than their predicament for a change.

This morning, she was seriously regretting those last few straight ones – as she looked, blurry eyed, into the mirror, at her ailing face. Back in the kitchen, she plugged her mobile phone into its charger; a little downcast that it hadn't rang the night before. As she decided that Conor had most likely been working most of the night, the phone actually did begin to ring, vibrating wildly on the kitchen counter. She rushed at it, partly because its piercing ring-tone was severely penetrating her throbbing head – and mostly because she hoped it was Conor.

Glancing down, she saw that it was Sheila, one of her girlfriends from London.

She hesitated a moment and then answered the phone, and Sheila's animated London accent bellowed down the line. "Lisa babe. How are you?"

"Hi Sheila – I'm alright. It's great to hear you", she said, sounding a little forced due to her hangover.

"You sound rough my love" noted Sheila and she laughed loudly. Lisa smirked. Her friends knew her all too well. "Yeah, … I got a bit too well acquainted with a bottle of vodka last night, and now I'm paying for it".

The two women chatted briefly as Lisa tried to suppress any worry in her voice, as well as ignoring the sharp pain in her head.

It transpired that Sheila was actually ringing her from the soft-leather comforts of her BMW coupe, as she sped down the M25 on her way to Dover. Knowing that Sheila was too far on the road to turn back, Lisa decided she would just have to deal with it. And would certainly wait until she arrived, to fill her in on the Bryan Wilks thing… but only if she really had to …and by being very economical with the truth, of course.

Sheila informed her that she was not on her own and that Caroline was actually sitting beside her – but couldn't take the phone as both her hands were dangling out the window, drying her nails.

"Hi Li" came Caroline's strained voice in the background.

Lisa laughed. That was typical Caroline, who was desperately scattered and was forever doing things at the last minute. Having studied the classics with Lisa in Roehampton, she was well educated, but generally had her head in the clouds, or stuck in some magazine. Her family were also rather well off and although she left her last job twelve months previous, she volunteered regularly for charity work in London's countless shelters. She was a kind-hearted creature and Lisa loved her for it.

Sheila, on the other hand, was a shrewd and strikingly beautiful woman who worked as a full time journalist with The London People. She was kind, yes, but ruthless if need be and her sharp mind had secured her some very exclusive stories over the past few years. Lisa had a deep respect for Sheila who had most definitely not hailed from a wealthy family background, but instead had worked hard to reach the level of prosperity that she now enjoyed.

As she ended the call, Lisa wondered how she might manage to keep the girls away from Sharon …and away from the ongoing mess. If she were to avoid Sharon, maybe she could also avoid having to tell any more lies.

It was one thing lying to the police, and having to lie to Conor, but it was quite another having to lie to her very best friends that she had known and loved for years; she prayed she wouldn't have to.

Chapter 28

When Lisa drove down to the Marine Parade to meet the two women, there followed a few moments of joyful reunion. Sheila ran her fingers through her cropped plum hair and looked out at the busy comings and goings of the waterfront.

Despite the overcast skies and the unsettled waters that the last couple of days' gloomy weather had brought, the port was as functional as ever; with lots of people moving around, each preoccupied with their own particular affairs. Gulls cried hungrily over their heads and the sea's wonderful salty smell filled their nostrils.

"God its lovely here" sighed Sheila.

Caroline was struggling to get her handbag out from the back of the car. "Damn phone keeps ringing and I can't find the blooming thing", she said as she grappled with the strap of her Louis Vuitton, which was entangled in the seat belt.

"What brings you two all the way out here then?" asked Lisa of her two friends.

"Had to see how you were getting on didn't we?" replied Sheila. "It's been almost a month now... and we've only had a couple of phone calls...what happened about that Irish guy you were after?"

Lisa laughed. "Come on... lets get lunch and I'll tell you all about it".

As Caroline finally freed her purse, and they locked the car, Lisa noticed the small travel cases in the back and she flagged a little. They were obviously staying longer than a couple of hours. Normally, this would have been wonderful; now however she began to sweat.

The people who knew her best were bound to be able to tell when she was lying.

* * * *

In 'The Port-Hole', which Lisa was really growing very fond of, the three women sat down at the table nearest the window, overlooking the Market Square'.

"Its so pretty here isn't it?" said Caroline, as she looked out at the water feature and two little children who played happily near it.

"Yeah gorgeous" replied Lisa.

"So come on then missus" began Sheila. "Tell all… have you heard anything from Ben yet?"

Lisa shook her head. "Ben hasn't so much as text me since I left the apartment. Instead he has been telling everyone that I'm suffering from some class of nervous breakdown. Even my mother thinks I'm here on a holiday to sort myself out… I don't mind though because it keeps everyone off my back about the marriage thing… for the time being".

"Don't you miss London?" asked Caroline.

"No… Hey I'm only a couple of hours away you know… Well, I miss you guys of course. And I guess the last few days, I have been thinking about home a lot… but life here is really nice. It's not slow paced at all - it's so, so busy. There are forever crowds passing through… all day, every day. But then the cottage I'm renting is removed from all that so I have the best of both worlds really…I'm able to concentrate on my writing".

An attractive teenage girl appeared beside them to tend the table. She wore the same embroidered polo shirt as the bar staff but had a neat little white apron tied around her waist. She clutched a docket book and smiled kindly at the women. "Ready to order?" she asked

Sheila ordered the chowder, Caroline wanted a ploughman's salad plate and Lisa just asked for a strong black coffee… her stomach was still iffy.

Sheila took out a packet of cigarettes and a shiny gold lighter. She held one out for each of the two women. Caroline shook her head. "For Gods sake, how long have you known me?" she sniped at Sheila.

"Sorry, just being polite…."

"You mean, you just keep forgetting, …" retorted Caroline.

Lisa took one and held it between two French polished fingernails as Sheila flicked the flame on. "…And hadn't you given up as well?" asked Caroline crossly.

Shelia groaned. "Oh for crying out loud mammy … Give it a rest".

Caroline grunted and began fiddling with her beer-mat.

"You're right I did give up…" answered Lisa "…but I've been having quite a lot of sneaky ones lately…its probably the stress of my marriage and everything…"

Caroline smiled sympathetically at Lisa. "Poor thing…" she said gently, reaching across the table and patting her arm, compassionately.

Shelia grinned behind her cigarette - knowing only too well, that Lisa had been having 'sneaky' ones for the last few years. Caroline had remained blissfully unaware of that one.

"Actually you do look a bit stressed Lisa…" continued Caroline.

"Do I? Yeah… well a hangover as bad as mine will do that to you" she answered warily, trying to perk up a bit – not wanting to cast any suspicion on her state of mind whatsoever.

The women spent a good hour chatting and catching up on any gossip. Lisa filled them in on her escapades with Conor. They were pleased that she seemed to have found someone she liked so soon and were eager to meet him.

"I just adore Irish men", said Caroline "I think it's their

accents".

"Mmm…" added Sheila. "…Especially men from Donegal. Now that accent sends shivers down my spine".

The women mused silently over that for a moment.

Meanwhile, the young woman came back to clear their table; her clattering of plates, interrupting their momentary reverie, and so Lisa decided to ask how long they were thinking of staying. When it became clear that the girls were considering an overnight jaunt, Lisa decided reluctantly she had better tell them about the drama next door.

"Listen" she began… "My neighbour that I told you about, Sharon… well… her husband went for a walk three nights ago…and didn't come home. He was depressed and they think he probably committed suicide up at the Cliffs"

"My God" started Caroline.
Sheila sighed aloud. "Poor woman… any sign of his body?"

"No nothing… I reckon she has accepted the worst now" Lisa lied. "…I just wanted to warn you about that - before we bump into her or something"

"Poor thing. Imagine losing your husband like that… you're life long partner… She is all on her own now … though she probably has family rallying around her at the moment"… considered Caroline.

"Well, no actually… not just yet. I think she had a falling out with her own parents a few years back, and she hasn't told his mother yet… she was to ring her today" replied Lisa.

"That's terrible" began a shocked Caroline. "Shouldn't we offer her around for some support?".

"I've been supporting her as much as possible… it was at Sharon's that I helped polish off that bottle of vodka last night. She is coping quite well really, considering. Anyway, if she wants to come round she can …but I think she might just want to be on her own at the moment".

Lisa already felt terrible lying, so blatantly, to her best friends… but it would be worse having to do it with Sharon around – and much worse still, if they were to discover the truth.

They drove back to the cottage.

* * * *

Sharon watched as the three women clambered out of their cars and walked into Lisa's place, chatting and laughing. She scowled. That's all they needed, even more outside influences.

Chapter 29

They sat around the quaint iron table in the sun-porch off Lisa's cottage. As the two cottages were identical in every aspect - except that each detail was like a mirror image, on the opposite side - this meant they could just about see into the corner of Sharon's porch. It was empty. Lisa found this very hard; considering Bryan's shadow had normally consistently moved around in there from morning till night while he was painting …while he was alive.

Now it stood dark, idle and distinctly ominous looking as far as Lisa was concerned - and a ripple of unease ran through her body.

The sun still hadn't managed to break through those stubborn grey clouds and Sheila shivered in anticipation of the storm that looked like it might rupture the moody skies at any moment.

"Looks so bloody miserable this evening doesn't it?" she noted, looking out one of the many large window panes in the porch, as Caroline hovered around, pouring coffee from the percolator jug; its wonderfully strong aroma wafting irresistibly around them.
"It's been scorching up until a couple of days ago", said Lisa slowly… "I don't think it's going to get any worse tonight though. Forecast mentioned sunshine again tomorrow so fingers crossed".
Sheila sighed in relief.

"Do you think you'll stay here Li?" asked Caroline, out of the blue.

Lisa looked once again towards the neighbouring porch and shuddered.

Suddenly she just wasn't sure.

As they continued to talk amongst themselves, Caroline glanced out the window. "Look… isn't that your neighbour? She's coming over"

The others looked. Sure enough, ambling across the grassy patch between the stone, wall and Lisa's cottage came Sharon's shapely form. Her long red hair was down this evening, cascading around her shoulders in a very dramatic fashion indeed.

Sheila looked across at Lisa. "Should we sympathise or what?" she asked. Lisa shrugged her shoulders. "I guess", she answered, hushing the girls, as Sharon got closer.

Lisa got up and opened the door to the sun-porch as Sharon approached.

"Sharon… how are you? Any news?"

Sharon shook her head. She spoke; her voice was weak – barely audible. "Nothing I'm afraid. They are continuing to search, apparently someone thought they saw something this morning but it turned out to be nothing. The Coastguard's lifeboat will continue to patrol the waters …just in case he floats back to the surface anytime soon".

Caroline jumped up, with arms outstretched. Clasping Sharon's hand between both of hers, she immediately began to offer her condolences. "I'm so sorry to hear about your husband" she started. "What a bloody awful thing for you to be going through…Sit down and have a cup of coffee. My God you're hands are cold… come on. This will warm you up".

Sharon smiled weakly at the friendly woman, and submissively allowed herself to be led to the table. "Sharon this is Caroline" introduced Lisa "and this here is Sheila. They're friends of mine from London. Came down to check up on me, I reckon".

Sharon heaved a sigh. "God …I'm sorry that you had to arrive slap bang in the middle of my nightmare…" she began, and her eyes glistened. "It'll affect your break now no doubt, especially with Lisa being … well, Lisa has been terrific - a real rock of strength for me".

Lisa looked down at her feet; shame engulfing her.

Sheila spoke with deep sincerity. "Don't be thinking about us and our stay…If there is anything we can do to help out while we're here, you let us know, Alright?"

"Thanks…" said Sharon and she brought the mug of coffee to her lips. It was warm and comforting.

Lisa felt increasingly ill at ease by the amount of concern that was being displayed. 'If only they knew' she thought. She sat down on the window ledge near Caroline. "Sharon, did you get in touch with your family yet? Or Bryans parents?" she asked.

"Yeah I did. I rang my mother first. That was interesting seeing as we have barely spoken to each other in almost ten years. She never really approved of Bryan and well… we drifted I guess. She *was* sorry though – I could hear it in her voice…" she gazed distantly into the murky brownness of her coffee, before continuing slowly. "…Not much point in her being sorry now though is there?"

Sheila threw Lisa a concerned glance and Lisa acknowledged it with a similar look of despair.

Sharon continued. "…But the hardest was ringing Bryans mother. She cried and cried – saying how she had put off her summer visit because of her sore ankle, and now she had missed out on ever seeing her boy again. She was so distraught. I felt so bad… I mean…. I felt bad being the one to tell her…She'll be arriving tomorrow morning, to help arrange the service".

"What service?" Lisa asked nervously.

"The service" said Caroline sharply.

"Oh…" replied Lisa. "The service – only I guess I thought that – well – I suppose I didn't think actually".

"Its okay Lisa" said Sharon reassuringly. "…I'll be having a religious service, in his memory. To see him on his way I guess"

Immediately, Lisa felt just terrible. His murderer was arranging a service to 'see him on his way'? For credibility or not, that was appalling. She felt sick. A dizzy sensation settled in behind her eyes.

She must have looked as bad as she felt, as Sheila immediately reached to put a cold palm to her forehead. "You alright babe?"

"You look like you've seen a ghost"

* * * *

Chapter 30

Cars' tyres could be heard crunching on the pebbles outside Lisa's bedroom window. She yawned and stretched. She could hear the hum of the shower in the bathroom and presumed that the girls were already up.

Sun was trying to stream in through the cracks in her curtains; the weather must have turned nice again, she decided and, for a moment, …she felt really good.

…But then …she remembered.

Sighing, as that, now familiar, feeling of despondency washed over her once again, she walked over and pulled back a tiny edge of curtain to see whose car was outside. Two women were getting out of a people-carrier, each with sunglasses on and one with a distinct limp. Their faces were serious; troubled looking, and Lisa instantly guessed they were Bryans mother and perhaps an aunt or sister.

Sighing, she stood back and went to her dressing table. She started to brush her hair. Looking into the mirror, she decided that she almost didn't recognise the woman staring back at her; She had become a liar and a deceiver. Not just a petty liar – like the white lies she would have told her friends from time to time, or the somewhat more substantial lies she had told her husband in the past, or the tale she was presently spinning her family about her marriage – no, she was no longer just a small-time deceiver – but a bona fide criminal. The guilt from which, during the last four nights of tossing and turning, was attributing to seriously baggy, eyes, a gaunt expression and a sick stomach.

Conor had called round to visit Lisa the night before. Sharon had stayed rather quiet – eventually making her apologies and heading home. Sheila and Caroline were suitably impressed by Conor; they had fawned over him for over an hour while drinking copiously from some vintage bottles of wine that they had brought with them – making distinct gestures of approval behind his back and squealing in delight when he finally placed kisses on each of their cheeks before leaving for work. He had winked and smiled knowingly at Lisa on his way out the door …and she had consequently began to tremble in anticipation of seeing him again.

Thinking about him now made her smile broadly, despite herself, and she continued to brush her hair.

Over breakfast, the two girls gushed about how impressed they had been with Conor. "I can see why you are so attracted to him Lisa…. He is really gorgeous", stated Caroline as she looked, with some hesitation, at the gristle protruding from her bacon butty. "…And so sweet and gentlemanly and friendly …and that accent" she continued.

Sheila, whose stomach was distinctly stronger in a hangover, took a large bite from her butty and chewed happily. "Mmm, he is lovely" she agreed, her mouth full. "Are you going to tell Ben about him?".

Lisa shook her head. "God no… well, not unless I absolutely have to for some reason" Sheila nodded in agreement. "Yeah, that might be just too much for poor old Benjamin. …Might push him right over the edge… oh I didn't mean… sorry" she said sheepishly as Caroline looked daggers at her. Lisa grinned a little. "It's fine. It wasn't my husband that jumped… I didn't even know him that well".

Caroline spoke tentatively. "Yeah but Lisa… if you don't

mind me saying, you do seem to be rather affected by the whole thing… You're not exactly yourself", she noted quietly – and she pushed her sandwich away from her – her stomach being decidedly disagreeable.

"Really? Well, I'm sorry, girls. I've become, in some ways, close to Sharon over the past few weeks and I guess …I pity her. This whole thing has affected me I suppose – it feels very close to home you know – I've never known anyone who committed suicide before".

Sheila smiled. "You'll be fine", she promised. "I know what its like – I've seen plenty of suicides – dead bodies – murders. The first few really shake you and then after that – it's a horrible way of thinking but - well, you become, sort of, accustomed to it."

Lisa smirked. "Well I don't plan on becoming accustomed to it thank you very much. One suicide is quite enough for me…Look, I'm sorry if I've been a bit off…" she apologised. "No problem" said Sheila.

"I'm just sorry about the breakfast you cooked…" started Caroline "…but I really can't face it" she grimaced.

The other two laughed at her pained face.

Deciding to leave Sharon and her mother in law to their own devices, Lisa and her two friends went on an exploration expedition. They wanted to see for themselves the 'Grand Shaft' that they had heard so much about and perhaps visit the Dover museum.

The women went, on foot, up the Western Heights from the cottage, to finally reach the Barracks. These 'Barracks', dated early 19th century, which was linked to the town via the Grand Shaft, were built on the White Cliffs, above Snargate Street – on Dover's seafront. Lisa had visited the Shaft before, with Sharon.

She walked now, down the steps of the slope towards the

opening of the Shaft.

"The soldiers that lived in these Barracks, used the Shaft as a means of getting to the Harbour quickly in emergencies" she shouted back.

The opening to the Shaft, comprising of a cylindrical tunnel, made of concrete, that descended through the Cliffs and was surrounded all the way down by three separate sets of steps, emerged in front them. They looked down into its looming darkness and Sheila smirked. "Great idea but I'd hate to have had to use it in an emergency – especially at night. It looks bloody scary down there…"

Caroline looked at her friend, bemused. "You? Scared of something? Hardly" she uttered sarcastically. Sheila replied with an irritated grunt.

Standing back while still looking towards the opening, Caroline stumbled over something and fell backwards, landing roughly on her backside. "Ouch – Oh for Gods sake… what was that?" she asked rubbing her lower back. "You fell over an old signpost. Its just a warning sign - to keep a safe distance from the opening" said Sheila as she tried to straighten the wooden post. "Should have warned you to keep a safe distance from the sign" she laughed.

"You alright?" Lisa asked as she helped Caroline to her feet. "Yeah I think so… I've broken it now have I?" she said of the post.

"Wouldn't worry about it", said Lisa as she spied the rotting woodworm infested timbers of the small sign. "I'll ring someone from the Council this evening and let them know…". She picked up her bag again. Sheila sniggered as Caroline dusted herself down.

"This main Shaft is 140ft deep", said Lisa, reading now from a pamphlet that she had brought with her. "…And it is some 26 ft in diameter. Each staircase has 140 steps…winding down behind each other to the very bottom…." She looked up. "Sharon and I climbed the steps a couple of weeks ago – we started at a doorway at the bottom… on Snargate Street – so that's where we would come out".

"Right so" began Sheila, who was determined to cover up her blunder of mentioning 'fear' in front of Caroline, and so she headed off resolutely to the closest set of steps. "Come on" she shouted back.

The other two followed, a little less confidently.

While the three 'explorers' scrambled their way in semi-darkness down the concrete steps, Sharon was sitting in her kitchen opposite her mother in law and Bryans' aunt, who were sipping coffee and snivelling. "How will you cope without him?" asked his mother. "How will any of us cope without him?".

Sharon sighed. "I don't know Clarissa. I guess we just will… eventually. It will take time I suppose".

Clarissa's sister picked up a handkerchief and proceeded to blow her nose loudly. "I feel so sorry for you Sharon. Here all on your own. Will you come back to Reading with us? You can stay with me if you like?"

Sharon got up to refill the kettle. "Thanks Annie. I appreciate that. To be honest, I don't know what I'll do. Maybe I'll stay in Dover. Bryan loved it here and I do too. It would be lonely alright…" she gazed out into the back garden.

Clarissa looked up. "Have you spoken to your mother? Maybe now would be a good time for you both to… well …to reunite. You could probably use a mothers love right now".

"There have been plenty of times that I could have used a mothers love in the past ten years Clarissa… and you have always been the one to show me it. I don't think she will come rushing down here if that's what you mean…"

Clarissa smiled sympathetically at Sharon. She had always been fond of Sharon. Bryan had certainly loved her.

Taking a deep breath, she sat up straight. "Sharon, we had better get started on this service. When do you think we should have it?"

"Well, I spoke to the local Catholic Priest this morning. He said he would be more than happy to hold one tomorrow if we wanted. He said that without …" she seemed to struggle with the words. "Without …a body…it really doesn't matter where or when we hold it. He said that, by right, he really should be holding it on consecrated ground but I thought that maybe he might say a few words here – in our back garden. I know that Bryan wasn't the most religious person in the world, but he would have liked that. He loved our garden – would stare at it from the porch while he painted…"

"Here sounds perfect. We can set up some chairs out the back and say a few dignified words in his memory", said Annie with a smile on her face.

Clarissa nodded.

"Right" said Sharon. "I'll ring the Priest then".

Chapter 31

A flashy red sports car, roared along the Marine Parade, before turning into the town centre and pulling up in an alleyway behind the Market Square. It stopped opposite 'My Way', the most recently established and ultra-modern women's clothes shop in Dover. The door opened and a long, slim, stocking-clad leg, appeared - its' pointy leather sandal, brashly quenching the smouldering butt of a cigarette beneath it onto the pavement. The body that emerged, dressed in a black, knee length, pencil skirt, and smart, tailored jacket, was that of the acutely conspicuous Riana Beaumont. A young and successful entrepreneur, she was the sole, proud owner of two women's Boutiques, the first based in Dover, the second in North West London.

She strode assertively towards the door of the shop and pushed it in.

The bell tinkled. "Morning Riana" came a woman's voice from inside and Riana disappeared inside the building.

* * * *

After their trip down the, somewhat, daunting, abyss of the 'Grand Shaft' and following a brief stint at the Dover Museum, where Lisa spent some time gathering information for her book, the three women had keenly decided to get some lunch. The weather was much finer today and so they had chosen to sit themselves at one of the few wooden tables outside 'The Port-Hole'; sipping willingly from halves of Fosters, eating club sandwiches and taking in what little sun they could, before the fickle forecast changed again.

The same pleasant young woman was at work there today;

floating around, gathering glasses and wiping away sticky beer spills from the few surrounding tables. She smiled at them as she passed - and Lisa thought how forthcoming she was.

As they sat, contentedly munching and sipping, Lisa's phone began to ring from within the depths of, what she called, her 'everyday' handbag – a large, turquoise-leather shoulder bag, purchased from one of the high street stores on Oxford Street, at the beginning of last year's summer season. She loved it. Sheila and Caroline grinned as she hastily began pulling out numerous accoutrements. She had placed an entire array of excessive, female paraphernalia, on the table before finally finding her mobile phone, at which time, naturally, it had stopped ringing. Flicking through its menu, she realised that it had been Sharon, trying to reach her. "I'd better ring her back", she said to the two girls.

They nodded, mouths full.

Lisa stepped up and walked away from the table, smiling at her friends - while inwardly, her heartbeat quickened with tension, as she waited for the phone to answer. Sharon's voice came on the line, wavering and shaky.

"Lisa – the service is tomorrow at one. I've asked Fr. Matthews to say a few words, in our back garden. Will you be there?"

Lisa turned away and lowered her voice to a forced whisper.

"Sharon, this is sick. You're holding a service in the very house where he was …where he died. This is all getting too much for me. The lies… the constant bloody lies" she inhaled deeply, as if to steady her self. Sharon immediately tried to re-assure her. "Lisa, calm down…listen to me. I don't like this any more than you do but once this is over, then that's it! Please, do this for me. I need you to be there tomorrow. ….. I …I can't do this on my own".

Lisa sighed. She glanced back at the girls who were now chatting to each other; paying no heed, whatsoever, to her conversation. She turned away again.

Whispering cautiously, she continued. "Sharon, there has to be an end to this… I can't stand it! You say you can't do this on your own but it's so damned unfair to insist on doing it with me. It should have nothing to do with me… and you shouldn't even be discussing this over the phone … God knows who could hear us talking or… where are you anyway?"

"I'm at home; don't worry, I'm on my own. Bryans mother arrived first thing - and her sister Annie, but they've gone for a stroll down by the Marina right now, to clear their heads… so… look… Lisa, this is the last thing I'll ask of you I promise".

Lisa sighed again, even more loudly. The two girls looked up and she gave them an assuring wave. She felt so trapped. She knew that Sharon was probably very genuine about needing her there; Lisa being the only other person to share her sinister secret; however, it was wrong of Sharon to keep dragging her into a mess that she wanted absolutely nothing to do with. Perhaps she would have to seriously consider returning to London after all.

…Then there was Conor. Yet another complication her life had decided to throw into the equation - for good measure.

Reluctantly, she agreed to be at the service, ended the call and sat down again with her friends.

"The service is tomorrow. I guess I'd better be there" she said, irately stuffing an olive into her mouth.

* * * *

The three women stood in the kitchen, huddled around the window, trying not to look too conspicuous, as they watched Sharon's mother-in-law hobble around outside, instructing the two elderly gentlemen who were spreading out plastic seats in the back garden. Having borrowed the chairs that morning, from the Town Hall, they were now placing them in straight rows, along the lawn. Folk had already begun arriving – many that appeared to be members of Bryans' family, someone that might have been Sharon's sister, and some of their mutual friends.

Respectfully attired in a black trouser suit, Sharon wandered around, shaking hands and snivelling on cue.

Lisa felt sick to the stomach.

Caroline and Sheila were going home today, after the service. They had packed their travel bags and were ready to leave Dover as soon as possible; Sheila already having received a few 'animated' phone calls from head office.

Caroline watched with concern as Lisa's pale face continued to stare indolently out the window. "Lisa. Are you sure you're okay?" she asked. Sheila stood back to light a cigarette and Lisa automatically held out her hand for a smoke. Sheila obliged.

"I'm fine" she replied, gazing still at Sharon's exhibition of heartache and woe.

"…I'm absolutely fine".

But Caroline wasn't convinced. She looked despairingly at Sheila in the background; who merely shrugged her shoulders, holding the fag between her lips to light it.

A knock echoed around the kitchen and Caroline went to answer it. She came back into the kitchen followed by Conor, whose smile brought an instant flush of colour, to Lisa's neck and cheeks. "Hi" she said eagerly, as he put an arm around her waist. "…Thanks for coming".

He grinned. "No problem…" he turned around "So how did you enjoy your few days in Dover then?" he asked of the two women. Caroline was busy wiping down the countertop and Sheila sat puffing and fiddling idly with her mobile phone. "Oh great -thanks" said Caroline with a beam. "Yeah it was good to see Lisa again", said Sheila. "We miss our luncheon rendezvous', don't we Li?" she continued.

Lisa smiled. "Yes we do… we really do. It was good to catch up. Now come on – lets get this over with".

Conor helped pull her chocolate-brown, Bolero around her shoulders and she smiled up at him with gentle eyes.

He kissed her tenderly on the forehead.

Despite himself, he was falling for her.

* * * *

Outside, Sharon looked anxiously towards her neighbouring cottage. She was relieved to finally see Lisa come meandering out, towards the stile in the wall; followed closely by Conor, and shortly behind them, her two London friends.

Too many people, she thought. Nice girls - but the sooner they left, the better.

Chapter 32

Fr. Matthews' poignant words floated evocatively around the garden; his deep voice resonating in the hearts of the bereaved, especially, Lisa presumed, in Sharon's, who, with immense difficulty evident on her face, had to sit and listen to how marvellous a person her husband had been. Sharon herself didn't speak; she said it would be too harrowing an experience, but Bryans mother struggled, on her sore leg, to the makeshift podium; sharing her regret and her mournful reflections with the people. Lisa's stomach continued to churn relentlessly, as she listened, with some distress, to the disturbing oration. A lump formed in her throat and her eyes began to sting.

Unexpectedly, she realised, she was crying.

As the final words were spoken, and folk began to get up and walk around, sipping from glasses of wine, chomping sandwiches and nibbling from homemade skewers of cheese-squares and grapes, Lisa felt a wave of nausea wash over her – she picked up her handbag and rushed back to the cottage; a concerned Conor in tow.

She hurried in through the front door and up the small wooden stairs to the bathroom. Conor arrived in time to hear the bathroom door bolt shut. He stood at the bottom of the stairs. "Lisa – you ok?" he asked.

Hearing a lurching sound, followed by coughing, he gathered that she was being sick and shrugged his shoulders at the two girls who had come running after them. Caroline went upstairs to knock on the bathroom door.

Sheila took hold of Conors hand and led him into the kitchen. "Come on, sit down and have a cuppa", she said calmly, while walking to the kettle.

"Is she sick? Has she caught something?" he asked. Sheila shook her head. "I don't think so… but I don't think she's ever been so close to a suicide situation before. It's obviously affected her"

Conor seemed confused. "She didn't even know the guy – she'd only met him about twice and… well, she said she wasn't his biggest fan. I don't know why it would upset her so much"

Sheila sighed. She sat down beside Conor and placed a mug of coffee in front of him. "This kind of experience can affect people in all sorts of ways. Maybe it reminds her of something or someone or maybe it just feels too close to home – being right next door and all"…

Sheila stirred in some sugar to her coffee and watched Conor as he shook his head in doubt.

"Unless she's pregnant", she added as a humorous afterthought. The shock on Conors' face made her giggle. "Oh relax – I'm joking…. You're face though…".

He smiled half-heartedly. "Well, whatever it is, I hope she's okay" he finished.

At that point, they were joined by Caroline and, a shook looking, Lisa who had caught the tail end of their conversation. "I'm absolutely not pregnant!" she began; darting a disapproving glare at Sheila. "…Really though you guys, I am so sorry. I don't know what came over me. I just felt all queasy and…"

"Don't worry about it" said Sheila.

"Are you okay?" asked Conor, standing up to let Lisa sit down. She smiled in appreciation. "Yep, I'm okay now …Thanks".

He placed a comforting hand on her shoulder and she immediately relaxed a little under his strong, warm touch.

* * * *

Sheila piled the bags into the tiny back seat of her Coupe and Caroline walked between the car and the wall to gaze once more at the dramatic view of the rolling sea.

Lisa smiled at them. "It was great to see you both. Thanks for coming all the way out here".

Sheila grinned at her "Oh its not that far away. We loved it here – we'll definitely be back". She began straightening her jacket and dangling her car keys in front of Caroline. "Come on Missus, let's go".

Caroline's blonde hair flew haphazardly around her face in the light breeze, as she turned to face Lisa. "Are you sure you're okay?" she asked gently. Lisa nodded, looking sideways at Conor. "Don't worry about me Caroline – I'm being well looked after".

"Well I hope so", said Caroline with a playful warning tone.

Conor grinned. "Don't know about that" he said "…but I'll do my best".

Caroline looked relieved.

"Thanks for having us" she said as she kissed Lisa on the cheeks. "It was nice to meet you Conor… maybe we'll see you again soon".

Conor nodded.

"Crikey you don't change…. Are you coming or what?" Sheila hollered from inside the car. "OI, keep you're hair on" retorted Caroline as she waved goodbye and jumped in beside Sheila.

The car sped off, beeping twice as it approached the descent and disappeared from view.

Conor and Lisa sauntered back into the cottage. They could still see figures moving around in Wilks' back garden as members of family continued to rally around Sharon.

Back in the kitchen, Lisa turned to Conor. "Are you working tonight?" she asked. He shook his head. "Nope".

"Then would you mind joining me for a drink…now? God knows I could do with one".

117

"Now? It's two in the afternoon. That's starting a bit early isn't it?"

"Well, the way I'm feeling….", she paused. "Ok, it is a bit early…"

Conor looked at her anxious eyes. He didn't know what was bothering her so much today, but he was worried about her. "Ok, come on then. I'll buy you a large one …and some lunch though".

She grinned.

Back, once again, in 'The Port-Hole', the staff were becoming accustomed to seeing Lisa and they smiled amiably at her as she came in. "Afternoon you two" said the young woman. "Hi Sasha" she replied, having overheard her name in conversation the previous afternoon.

Sasha moved around them to behind the counter. "In for some lunch?" she asked as she topped a pint of Guinness for the gentleman in the corner, who was sitting with his back to them. "Yea, a liquid lunch" said Lisa with a smirk.

"…And we'll see a menu too. She's not a complete alcoholic…" quipped Conor. He turned to Lisa. "You need to line the stomach before a day of drinking you know".

"Who said anything about a day of drinking?" she asked cheekily.

"Come on, from the way you were talking? Anyway, I can smell a good session from miles away…" he laughed.

They ordered two drinks and sat down with the lunch menu, at the table near the window, and looked out. The sun had sneaked in behind a band of clouds and so what had started as a sunny morning, had turned into a rather overcast evening.

Sasha arrived with their drinks. The young barman, who Lisa had seen on her very first night in The Port-Hole, came in and sat at the counter. He had the daily papers and began flicking through them. He saluted them as he caught their eye and they gestured hello back to him. Lisa watched as Sasha moved closer to him and they shared a joke. He reddened as they giggled. 'They definitely fancy each other' she thought to herself. She sipped her gin; Conor merely looked at his pint.

"Are you going to look at it or drink it?" asked Lisa after a few moments.

"All in good time" he said as he watched the velvety stout swirl around, slowly settling to black.

He looked up, hesitating slightly. "…Lisa, are you okay? I mean… did this whole suicide thing really get to you? I was worried about you this morning"

She looked to the table and began to fidget with her beer-mat. "Yeah for some reason, it has gotten to me. I don't know why". She was lying; she hated lying. She looked up at him again. He was staring anxiously at her.

"I don't have a friend who committed suicide or anything like that… It hasn't reminded me of anything… I'm just having a problem dealing with it. I'll be fine".

Conor wasn't convinced. He planted his palm around the cool pint glass and brought the creamy Guinness to his lips.

'He didn't understand her but he wanted to help her'.

Chapter 33

As the evening rolled out in front of them, and the drinks continued to flow, Lisa's mood became decidedly lighter. Her head was swimming and as she looked into his smiling face, she wondered was it the warmth of the alcohol or the warmth of her emotions that had her tingling inside. She was so surprised at having discovered what, in fact, felt very like 'love', only mere weeks after having immersed herself in her new life – if only she hadn't also encountered Sharon and her grave predicament, her heart would have been singing right now.

It was nearing eight o'clock – Conor glanced at his watch. He knew that Lisa could really do with going home and getting some well-earned sleep. "Come on, lets call it a day", he said, slurring slightly. He stood up to go and Lisa put out her hand. "No, stop... wait. I've something to tell you".

She hiccupped.

"Come on Lisa… not now…lets get you home"

"Yes now Conor… now sit back down … Please"

He detected the slight urgency in her voice, despite her inebriated state; Conor sat back down.

"What is it? What's wrong?"

She put her hand across the table and grabbed hold of his arm. "Conor – I…. I know something. Something that I shouldn't – and it's driving me crazy". She stopped and put a hand to her forehead. "God what am I saying…. This is not a burden I should be sharing with you… its just…"

Conor looked closely at her; suddenly feeling rather sober.

"Lisa – what's the matter?" he asked tenderly.

She shook her head and tears glistened once again in her eyes. "I shouldn't be telling you this… but it's eating me up inside".

"You can tell me anything you want" he started. "…I know we've only been seeing each other for a bare week but … but you can trust me".

She smiled. Even in her, somewhat waning, drunken state, she felt so close to him and despite what he said about barely knowing each other, she believed what he said to be true.

She leaned closer. "It's about Bryan Wilks. He… he didn't commit suicide".

"What?" he asked quickly.

She hesitated. "Ssshh" she hissed. "He didn't commit suicide. He was killed… by Sharon".

It landed like the unexpected blow from an old minefield. "Jesus Christ and His Holy Mother…. Do you know what you're saying Lisa?"

"Of course I bloody well know… I've been able to think of nothing else since it happened" she snapped.

Conor shook his head in disbelief.

"But the police… why haven't you told the police what you know? What about the search?"

"Listen… Conor - their marriage was a mess… a real mess. Bryan was a thug. He was hitting her. I didn't realise at first why she kept looking for excuses to leave the house but… then I saw the bruises… and they used to fight. I could hear them rowing from my house". She buried her head in her hands. Conor touched her arm comfortingly. He could see she was struggling with this.

"Go on"

"On the night of our walk to the marina, after you left, I heard a gun shot. I thought he had taken his abuse too far, I actually thought he had killed her but then…" Lisa looked around her. She reduced her whisper to one that was barely audible. "…Then she came round to my house, confessing that she had killed him… and begging me to keep quiet about it. I was determined that she should tell the police and that if she didn't then I would… but she was so persuasive. She *begged* me not to dob her in; that she couldn't *possibly* go to prison for him… and I finally gave in".

Conor was stunned. He couldn't believe what he was hearing. "You gave in? But Lisa… she killed him. She killed him and faked his suicide? This is really big… this is too big for us… we'll have to do something about this. We have a responsibility to do the right thing here"

"Conor – don't you see? It's gone too far. Of course I want to do something about it. Of course I want to *do the right thing* – Don't you think I've said all this to her already? I've thought about nothing else… I feel terrible. I am sick all the time and practically *drowning* in guilt… but if we tell the police now I'll be seen as having withheld vital information – aiding and abetting a murderer – an accessory – God knows what else… I know it sounds desperately selfish but I just can't do it – I can't let my father down like that…"

"What about the body?" he asked, almost fearfully.

She shrugged her shoulders. "I didn't ask… I didn't want to know".

"Well, that's something I suppose. The less you know the better".

Tears rolled down her cheeks now, smudging her mascara and running streaks through her light foundation. She looked a mess. Suddenly, she was a mess; appearing so vulnerable that all at once he felt an overwhelming urge to protect her.

He stood up and came around to her side of the table, pushing in on the bench beside her. Placing an arm around her shoulders he kissed her head.

"Don't worry – we'll sort this out", he said reassuringly – but without actually having any idea how.

* * * *

The barman had gone in behind the counter to work a shift. Having asked him to call a cab, they waited together outside the pub. Lisa thrust her hands into her pockets and shuffled her feet nervously. Conor was silent. He felt, that at the moment, he just didn't know what to say or do. In fact all the way home in the cab, he didn't know what to say and when they arrived at the cottage, he was still feeling as flummoxed as ever.

He was falling in love with this woman – but suddenly was she not the person he thought she was? She was embroiled in something very sinister – something that was much, much bigger than her. But deep down he knew that, regardless of all this, his feelings towards her hadn't changed.

When they settled down on her sofa, her tears came hard and heavy. He held her close. There was little else he could do; little other solace he could offer her.

So, instead, he just held her tighter.

Chapter 34

When she awoke, it took her a moment to realise exactly where she was. The room was darkened; the curtains closed. It was the ornately patterned wallpaper on the wall opposite her that clinched it – she rubbed her eyes and her pounding head. A blanket had been placed carefully on her lap. As she lay there, on the sofa, considering the hangover that was firmly settling in behind her eyes, all of a sudden she groaned loudly and pulled a cushion down over her face - as vague, fuzzy memories of her previous nights' 'heart to heart' with Conor, came crashing down on her aching brain.

She sat up, suddenly realising he was gone; that he hadn't been due in at work this morning, so he must have fled; waited until she fell asleep and then fled …out of shock …out of anger. He must hate her, for what she knew… and for what she *hadn't* done…. that being, of course, 'the right thing' …going to the police.

She fell back again, turning over, to bury herself into the sofas' brown upholstery. She lay there, wondering that, if she tried rubbing her eyes really, really hard, might she possibly wake up from this horrifying nightmare, once, and for all?

Just then, someone knocked on the front door.

She couldn't possibly answer it, not in this state…. But what if it was Conor?

Leaping up, with a great deal of haste and not enough consideration for her swirling head, she had to stand still for a moment, waiting for the room to stop spinning. She glanced quickly in the old mirror over the fireplace. Her hair was limp; her typically sallow skin, noticeably pallid and her eyes surrounded by dark rings and lacking any sparkle whatsoever, but suddenly she was just too distraught to give a damn - and so she pulled back the latch and opened the door.

It was Sharon.

"Oh, it's you" she uttered lethargically, turning around and shuffling, in her socks, to the kitchen.

"Oh very nice" said Sharon, offended.

She followed Lisa. "Are your friends gone then?" she asked, as Lisa filled the kettle and reached to the press for mugs.

"Yes" she replied, somewhat apathetically.

"Lisa I know yesterday was hard for you… I saw you leave… I wanted to follow you but how would that have looked? Look, its over now. The search for a body will continue but they know he committed suicide. Bryans' family have returned to Reading to sort out some of his affairs. They said they might return in a few days in case the search turns up something… I thought they might stay actually, but it seems they are finding it too hard. They wanted me to go with them but …" She paused and then changed direction. "Inspector White rang me this morning to see how I was feeling after the service. He apologised again for my loss… said he hoped we would have a body before long, to give him a proper burial …but the most important thing Lisa, is that he hasn't a clue… I really believe it's finally over".

Lisa turned around to look at her; Sharon was smiling… there wasn't any real pleasure there, but she was smiling and she shouldn't be…. Lisa gave a short, sickened grunt. She walked over to Sharon…. Holding her gaze, she whispered slowly. "…This …will never …be over". She continued to stare into Sharon's face for a moment… before turning away and returning to the kettle.

Sharon sighed and sat down. "Lisa, … you must hate me for putting you in this position".

"That, Sharon, is an understatement", Lisa snapped bitingly.

"Oh Look, …if you want me to bloody leave I will. I wouldn't blame you. I'm so sorry for coming to you for advice that night… for loading you with my problems. I'm sorry that any of this ever happened… that he ever hit me… that it came to such a gruesome end. I'm sorry". Her voice cracked and a tear ran down her face.

Lisa, despite her anger, hated to see someone cry and felt a surge of guilt.

Unsure, however, of whether this was genuine sorrow, or emotional blackmail of sorts it was a moment or two before she finally shook her head and spoke.

"No…you don't need to go Sharon… I hate being involved in this… but I don't hate you. … I sure hope you're right about this being over though".

She sat down opposite Sharon.

Sharon reached across the table and grabbed Lisa's hand in both of hers. She stared intently into Lisa's face. "Lisa. I know that so far as what happens in our heads, this will never truly end, but concerning the police? I promise you its over… It's our secret. No one will ever know… just you and me".

At this point Lisa pulled her hand free and covered her face with her palms. "No, Sharon" she began from behind her hands "… its not just you and me".

Sharon looked surprisingly calm; her voice lowered. "You've told your friends haven't you?", she said, as though she had half expected it.

Lisa looked out from between her fingers. "No… no I didn't tell them… they would have marched me straight to the police… I told Conor". Sharon seemed only vaguely taken aback, as though deep down she was never really expecting Lisa to manage to keep this to herself. "I didn't think you two had gotten that close in only a few days", she said.

"I know… I didn't either but… I guess I got carried away in the moment… We'd had a little to drink yesterday evening …and I just came out with it…"

Sharon got up and walked to the counter; she finished making the coffee that Lisa had abandoned.

Nothing was said for a few moments while Sharon filled the mugs and stirred in extra sugar. Lisa felt awkward, sitting with her back to Sharon; listening to the clinking of the spoon in each of the mugs.

"Sharon, say something" she said finally.

Sharon carried over the coffee and sat down. "There's no point in saying anything now is there? You've told him, so you can hardly ring him up and tell him it's all been a joke.… The ball is in his court now.… How did he take it?"

Lisa wrapped her hands around the warm mug and closed her eyes to the strong aroma. "He was shocked… didn't say much… reckoned of course that we did the wrong thing by not going straight to the police".

"But he's going to keep quiet, isn't he?"

Lisa hesitated. "…I don't know".

"You don't know? Surely it's in your best interests to know…"

"You mean *your* best interests" she retorted sharply.

Sharon sighed and nodded yieldingly.

Coming down from her defensive high ground, Lisa continued in a slow, drawl"…I must have fallen asleep on the sofa last night… he was gone when I woke up".

"Oh my God.… He could be at the police station right now then?"

"Oh relax… I don't think so Sharon… I mean… I don't know but… he's probably just a bit shaken by it all…"

"Shaken? Outraged you mean… appalled, I'm sure". Sharon was upset… Lisa drank down some coffee and got up for her cigarettes.

She threw one towards Sharon. "Well even if he is outraged and appalled, I really don't think he would go straight to the police with this. It could mean landing me into real deep waters too - and he thinks more of me than that... at least, I think he does".

With that, they heard someone cough and they looked up, startled.

It was Conor.

Chapter 35

"Your door was open. You should really be more careful about what you talk about with your door open... anyone could overhear you".

Lisa just looked at the floor... embarrassed.

He walked in and sat down.

He looked coldly at Sharon, who continued to puff at her cigarette, pale and concerned. "Bit of a mess Sharon..."

She raised and furrowed her brow in agreement, exhaling smoke slowly.

He continued crossly. "I think what you've done is wrong... I know you were a victim, I can even understand why you would be driven to kill him, but faking his suicide and involving an innocent person in your scheme, is so ...twisted" He shook his head at her in repugnance.

She looked at him, angry at first, but then yielding a little. She hung her head. "I know you're right... but it wasn't my intention to involve Lisa. That happened by accident... because I panicked... And the suicide story... that was panic too... total and utter panic – I wasn't about to go to jail for him Conor. You have no idea what I've been through ...none".

Conor shook his head. "No... No you see I've been thinking about this. I've thought about nothing else since Lisa told me.... And I reckon you're being a selfish bitch ...that you could have pulled the plug on this in time – pulled the self-defence card, you were duty bound to do the right thing – and when you didn't, Lisa was duty bound to do it for you - only that she let her emotions rule her head and now its too late... it's gone too far; what with wasting police time and the huge money spent by the search and rescue crews, you've made your position a lot worse. It's a lie gone out of control Sharon and that's why you won't go to the police. This shouldn't be left up to Lisa... or to me".

Sharon looked at him speechlessly.

Lisa felt awkward. "Conor, she did something really crazy and unfounded – but she was in a really bad place when it happened. She wasn't thinking straight and now she has to live with that for the rest of her life".

"For Christ's sake Lisa, why are you defending her? Look at you? You're an emotional wreck since this happened. You're a mess... and because of her selfishness, you have to live with this too, for the rest of *your* life" he looked to the table "... and now I will have to as well".

Sharon looked up quickly. "You mean you'll keep quiet?"

"Not for your sake..." he started. "But in case Lisa was to get caught up in the blame..." he turned to Lisa "...if its what you want Lisa... then I wont tell the police".

For a moment, Lisa didn't know how she felt. She had actually been slightly relieved that Conor knew – relieved that it was in someone else's hands – relieved that she had someone other than Sharon to confide in. Perhaps she was even hoping that *he* might 'do the right thing' and go to the police, taking the immediate burden from her. But he wasn't going to. He was too fond of her; she knew that.

"Thanks Conor. I'd appreciate it. It's just all so ... complicated".

Conor nodded. He looked at Lisa with caring eyes.

He desperately wanted to look after her.

Sharon, however, had sensed the intended hostility from Conor; hostility that she decided she could appreciate. She touched his arm.

"For what its worth Conor, thank you. Now… let's try and put this whole mess behind us, if we can". She got up. "I'll go. I've got some sorting to do".

"Sorting?" asked Lisa.

"Yeah, I'm going through Bryans stuff today. Going to try bringing some of his paintings to an art dealer in Calais tomorrow, Jacques something or other, that Bryan had been in touch with before he died. He was interested in buying some of them… Its not going to be easy, but I could do with the cash, …and with a break from this place".

"That's a bit soon isn't it?" asked Conor, worried about how suspicious it might look.

"As far as anyone is concerned I'm just going out there for a few days break, ok? She smiled weakly at Lisa, threw an appreciative nod in Conors direction, and left.

Conor looked at Lisa's apprehensive face. He put his arms around her, holding her close. "Don't worry. It'll be fine", he said quietly.

Lisa closed her eyes, hiding her face deep in the creases of his shirt; breathing in his musky aftershave and revelling, for a moment, in the sense of safety and security she felt from beneath his strong arms.

Chapter 36

Lisa sat, this sunny afternoon, watching as 'old John' and Conor heaved together, pulling up stubborn weeds from the small earthen patch at the front of the lawn. She had been doing some weeding herself but had decided it was too much like hard work and was sitting now, smiling as the men chatted and laughed – but inside, her heart was heavy and her mind troubled.

It was only a week, since the morning Conor had assured them he would keep their secret. Within those seven days, Lisa was perhaps beginning to feel a little bit more at ease with the situation, or at least with her personal involvement, which, as Conor kept pointing out, was minimal. But she was still struggling, daily with her private demons – feeling as though she were being submerged slowly, in a well of guilt and shame.

Looking now at Conor, she knew, that despite her instant love and appreciation for Dover, she would definitely have been on that motorway last week, returning sheepishly to London, with her tail between her legs, if it hadn't been for her 'knight with an Irish accent' – and her ever-growing fondness for him.

Sharon had remained in Calais for six days – her car had returned to its usual spot the previous night. Lisa glanced over at the cottage, which, having sat idle for the past few days now had its windows open, with a superb smell of cooking wafting across the lawns. Conor and John looked up. "Something smells good", noted John. "Sure does", agreed Conor as he wiped his forehead with the back of his gardening glove. Lisa threw her eyes to heaven. "Ok I get the hint; the workers are hungry" she laughed. The men bent over again, continuing with their work. Getting up to go back inside, Lisa was suddenly stopped short by the curvy, eye-catching figure of a woman, standing outside the wall.

"Hi, can I help you?" Lisa asked. The woman saluted her graciously, before then turning to the two hunched over figures behind the wall. "Hi Conor...." She said. Conor stood up straight, surprise evident on his face. "Riana?" he said. "When did you get back?".

Riana smiled and walked to the gate. "Last week" she said, glancing across at Lisa. "May I?" she asked, with her hand on the bolt. Lisa nodded hesitantly as the attractive lady, opened the gate and walked in. She and Conor hugged for a moment and Lisa felt a hot flush of jealousy rush through her body.

Conor turned around. "Lisa, this is a friend of mine, Riana Beaumont. She owns a boutique in town. Riana, this is Lisa". Lisa waited for him to say 'my girlfriend' but he didn't. Riana strode towards Lisa with her right hand outstretched. "Nice to meet you Lisa. I hope you don't mind me popping round today. I asked down at the Docks where I'd find him and they sent me up here...." She turned around. "By the way, uncle Joe is looking good" she said to Conor and he grinned. "I'll bet he was glad to see you".

Lisa's jealousy was really bubbling now; she hated that this mystery woman was so gorgeous; that she knew Conor so well and that she was friendly with his uncle. Lisa hadn't even met uncle Joe yet.

Looking from Riana's slim fingers, down at her own earth-coated, hands she immediately made a mental note to take an emergency slot at the beauticians the next morning. She had been so absorbed in everything over the past few days that she hadn't paid very much attention to her personal appearance and that wasn't like her.

Riana smiled broadly at them all; Lisa smiled back, gritting her teeth.

Inside, Lisa made some tea and a light lunch. Bringing the colourful salad plates to the table in the porch, she rolled her eyes, as Riana sat, cross legged, on the window ledge, throwing her long, deep brown, hair around as she chatted to an eager looking Conor. "Yes thank goodness business is great. I've been working day and night to promote the new shop and finally it's taken off". Conor nodded. "Riana went to London six months ago to set up her new boutique" he said, explaining to Lisa. "Mmm that sounds great", said Lisa, trying her best not to allow sarcasm sneak into her tone. She knew, that Riana would probably frown upon Lisa's independent wealth, as she was a lady who quite clearly worked hard for her cash. Instantly Lisa became concerned that Rory would see this woman's predisposition towards hard work as being a more favourable quality, than Lisa's rather 'silver spooned' existence.

As they ate, Lisa opened a bottle of wine and poured everyone a glass. She was determined now to appear gracious and sociable in front of Conor, she raised her glass - "To Riana's Boutiques" she stated. Conor beamed. "Absolutely… Riana's Boutiques" he repeated and Riana smiled modestly. "Thanks you Lisa".

John raised his drink also - and the four glasses clinked together above the iron, porch table. John wiped his mouth on his napkin. He smiled cordially cross at Lisa. "Thanks for lunch Lisa love… I have to go and see to some jobs at home. Look after this Irish rogue for me" he laughed. Conor stood up. "I'll walk you out John" he said and suddenly the moment that Lisa was dreading had arrived. She was alone with the lovely Riana.

Riana sipped from her wine glass and smiled awkwardly at Lisa. "So Lisa, you and Conor are an item then?"

Lisa nodded. "Yeah, we'll not long. We've been seeing a bit of each other over the past few days" she bit her lip for a moment and then decided to plunge straight in. "…. If you don't mind me asking, Riana, how do you and Conor know each other?"

"You mean am I an ex-girlfriend?" asked Riana.

"Well…" Lisa flushed with embarrassment. "Yes…actually". Riana smiled. "Relax Lisa. Yes, we went out briefly when Conor first came to Dover, but it didn't work out. Now we are good friends".

"Oh right…. Well. I'm glad we cleared that up. Sorry about asking like that"

Riana shook her head, her choppy fringe, flicking demurely across her big dark brown eyes. "Don't worry about it. I'd be asking too… if I was in your position".

They sipped uncomfortably at their wine, each wishing Conor would return.

"So, when did you arrive in Dover then Lisa?" Riana asked quickly.

"Oh only about 5 weeks ago… the end of May. I came out here to try my hand at writing…"

Riana seemed mildly interested.

"Oh that's nice… what have you written?"

"Well, nothing much yet, I haven't had much of a chance…a lot's been going on around here lately"

Riana sat forward. "My shop manager was raving about something this morning. She mentioned a suicide on the cliffs… that some guy jumped last week"

"Well it was more like ten days ago… but yeah a guy jumped alright. He lived right next door to me, with his wife".

Riana sat up with interest. "Right next door? You mean it was that funny painter guy?"

"Yeah that's right. Bryan Wilks"

"Wow… poor bastard. Wonder what drove him to that?"

"I… I don't know", stammered Lisa, immediately uncomfortable with the conversation. At that moment, Conor returned.

Chapter 37

For the rest of that desperately uncomfortable afternoon, Lisa sat, in distinct July heat, and listened as Conor quizzed Riana, and she continued to throw that illustrious brown hair around; laughing aloud, retelling stories and basically having a wonderful time, at what, Lisa believed, was her expense.

As time passed and it began to approach three o' clock, Riana glanced at her watch. "It's time I was going. Lisa… thanks so much for a lovely afternoon. Considering I just arrived on top of you like that… thanks again".

"No problem Riana. No problem at all" replied Lisa – the insincerity was evident in both women's voices, but not to Conor, who, being a typical male, thought everything was rosy and that it was wonderful to see the two women getting on so well.

"Listen Riana, why don't we all meet up in the pub tonight? We could have a few drinks together- catch up properly?" suggested Conor.

Lisa was appalled at the suggestion and immediately interjected. "I don't know Conor, my head is still aching from yesterday…."

She saw the look of disappointment on Conors face. Riana saw it too and started to smirk. "Not to worry… you can join us another night Lisa" she quipped.

Lisa frowned. "No… no that's fine. I'll get my glad rags on".

Riana smiled…. "Great… see you tonight then".

Conor waved at her as she strode back to her car, opened the door, manoeuvred her long legs back into the drivers seat and took off with a roar of the engine.

Lisa turned to Conor.

"Why would you do that?" she asked crossly. "Do what?" asked Conor.

"Invite an ex-girlfriend into my house and then to join us in the pub tonight?"

"Ah, you're jealous aren't you?" he asked mockingly. The serious look on Lisa's face turned his smile upside down. "Look Lisa, Riana is a nice girl but she is a friend… that's it. I get on well with her and you did too… I could tell… Come on… you'll enjoy yourself"

Lisa was disgusted at Conors blindness when it came to this woman, who clearly wanted to get back into his bed.

"If you insist on doing this, then you will be doing it on your own" she said, rather too confidently.

He looked at her… hurt and cross. "Fine" he said sharply.

"What?"

"I said 'fine'. If that's what you want… I've no intention of going back out with Riana… I know you and I haven't been seeing each other very long, but if you don't trust me then what can I say?"

Conor pulled his jumper back on over his sweaty, earthy t-shirt and walked out, closing the door roughly behind him.

* * * *

That evening, Lisa sat on the sofa in the sitting room, looking at the clock, glancing at mind-numbing rubbish on the television and thinking that she should have had her computer out instead of wallowing in self-pity over some man…. Only he wasn't just some man. She was in love with Conor – yes, even after only a few days, she was definitely in love with him - and she had just pushed him headlong into going to the pub, with his ex-girlfriend.

'Idiot, Idiot, Idiot' she thought as she slapped the sides of her head with her hands.

Sharon appeared at the sitting room door. "I knocked but you didn't answer, it was off the latch…why are you hitting yourself?".

Lisa looked up. "Oh don't mind me…", she said vaguely.

Sharon sat down on the edge of sofa beside her. "So, how've you been the last week?" she asked. Lisa shrugged. "Don't know… fine I guess"

Sharon nodded. "Good…" she said carefully.

Lisa picked up the remote and flicked off the television. Silence fell in the room.

"So how did you get on in France?" she asked Sharon eventually. "Oh ok Lisa – I think… I managed to sell three of his 'Scenes of Dover' pieces… they were his very best. He had been having trouble selling his more recent work… but these were good. I would take photos of places and he would paint them. He was excellent at scenes and landscapes and buildings … good at something I suppose" she paused.

"Good at knocking you about as well though wasn't he?" said Lisa sardonically – but she immediately felt bad. "Sorry Sharon" she said awkwardly. Sharon smiled. "Don't apologise… you're right … Anyway that money should tide me over for a bit. But I'll be returning to Calais in a couple of days with some more works to sell".

Lisa sighed. "That's good…." She looked up with tears in her eyes.

"Lisa I feel so responsible for your tears… I know you are still guilt ridden. If there was something I could do, I would"

"Its not that… well, I am still guilt-ridden but …it's Conor. He is going out tonight with his gorgeous, successful, entrepreneurial ex-girlfriend".

"He is? How come? Have you two had a row?"

"Not really - but instead of going with them like he suggested, I'm here, out of my mind with jealousy… and worry".

Sharon grinned. "Lisa… he is in love with you. A blind man could see it… you're worrying over nothing".

Lisa wasn't so sure.

Chapter 38

The Western Heights, or 'Forgotten Fortress' as folk sometimes referred to it, was truly living up to its ancient namesake as far as Lisa was concerned. In fact, she felt like something of a 'Forgotten Fortress' herself. Being embroiled in this sinister situation was, in fact, confining her in more ways than one. Afraid to return to London, to her friends and family, for fear of letting something slip, she was also afraid to stay, believing that every time she looked at Sharon's face, she was being cruelly reminded of what she knew – and every time she spoke to someone, other than Conor, she was having to hide behind her own 'built up walls', watching every word she spoke, for fear of blurting out the truth in a moment of weakness.

It was two days since Conors rendezvous with Riana. Lisa learned the following morning, through Old John, that they had all met up in 'his' local haunt, 'The Channell Stop', and had stayed there, drinking cosily, until midnight, instead of going to 'The Port-Hole' like she had presumed, and this incensed her immensely. Why there? Had it been a special place for them?

He hadn't been in touch all that day – not until that evening, when he had tried phoning her mobile, but she had purposefully let it ring; stubbornness overcoming curiosity; Anger overcoming concern.

Today, standing alone, back on Langdon Bay, trying to gather her thoughts, trying once again to catch a glimpse of 'The Summity' with her digital camera, she remembered the day that she and Sharon had sat up high on the cliff, trying to surmount the awkwardness that had lingered surrounding Sharon's 'bruises' – and a rush of bad feeling surged through her body.

She could see the bits of old timber and iron sticking up now through the lapping waters. As she poised herself to take a photo, her phone began to vibrate. 'Damn' she thought, she pulled the mobile from her pocket. It was Conor.

She answered it. "Hi Conor" she started. She was about to continue with an apology but Conor got in there first. "Lisa I'm sorry. I've been a right idiot… I shouldn't have spoken to you like I did. Can I call round?"

Lisa smiled. "Of course, but give me an hour. I'm not there at the moment".

An hour later, she sat in the kitchen, eagerly awaiting his knock on the door. When it came, she rushed to it. It had only been two days, but it had felt like a lifetime. When he stood inside the door, he put his hands on her waist and pulled her close. "Riana Beaumont is a nice woman, a friend – but she isn't a patch on you. I promise you I am not interested in her". Lisa smiled broadly, looking at him in breathless anticipation.

He kissed her passionately; she relished the tenderness of his embrace.

But, looking then down at his watch, he whispered in her ear. "I am so sorry that I can't stay but, its 11am and I promised Joe I'd head down to the office to help him with some paperwork… Can I come back later …to finish what we've started?"

She groaned. "Do you have to go now?"

He nodded.

"Oh ok then…"

He smiled at her and kissed her forehead. Heading towards the door, he leant over and picked something up. "You have a letter", he said turning the brown envelope over in his hands. "But doesn't your mail get left in the post box outside?"

She nodded curiously.

"It must have been hand delivered – no stamp", he pointed out as he handed the envelope to Lisa. "Strange" she said as she pushed her fingernail under the seal and tore it open.

Conor was about to turn and leave when he saw every ounce of colour drain very quickly from Lisa's face.

"What is it? What's the matter? Bad news?"

Lisa's hand began to shake and she dropped the paper to the floor, steadying herself from falling, by grabbing hold of the sideboard. Conor rushed to her aide.

As she stood there, trembling, he picked the paper up from the floor. It was a single piece of paper with one line written in scrawled handwriting across the centre of it.

'*Your secret's out Lisa*'.

Chapter 39

Allowing the distinctly piquant, aroma of Hennessy Brandy to infiltrate her nostrils and hoping that a generous measure might help to settle both her stomach and her nerves, she gulped it back, picked up the bottle and added another sizeable drop to her glass.

Conor scrutinized the note over and over again.

Lisa snorted. "Well someone clearly knows our secret... the game is up", she said caustically. Conor just looked at her. "This could be anything... this could be a practical joke or something – it might be someone who heard you mention something about 'a secret' and thought they'd give you a hard time..." he offered gently.

Lisa laughed affectedly. "I doubt it Conor. A bit too serious for that... and I know for a fact that Sharon hasn't breathed a word of this to anyone – she couldn't take the risk..." With that, Lisa suddenly stopped talking. She wiped her teary eyes and began to look intently at Conor. He stood up immediately. "Oh no... you aren't going to blame me for this I hope" he began.

She groaned. "It's her isn't it? You've told her and now she is getting me good".

"Getting you good? I've never heard anything so bloody ridiculous. You mean Riana don't you? Well, she wouldn't bother... she wouldn't be that childish - even if I had told her anything, which I haven't".

"You must have Conor... how else would this have happened? You are the only third party who knows any of this".

Conor looked hurt as Lisa ranted.

"You told her when you were out together I'll bet… maybe you were that drunk you don't even remember it? She wants you back Conor; it's as clear as day - and she is going to get me out of the picture to achieve it"

His eyes narrowed and darkened, and he turned to leave. On reaching the door, he turned back briefly. Quietly but seriously, he said, "I promised you Lisa… I don't break my promises".

"Conor what am I supposed to think? Conor…. CONOR?"

The door slammed. Lisa's lip quivered. She looked down at the scrap of paper; Conor had flung it to the floor on his way out. With shaking fingers she picked it up again and hastily scrunched it into a ball; she started to sob. Tears flowed fast down her cheeks; her heart ached – she was confused.

'Why would he have done this? And why then deny it? There was no way that Sharon would have let this slip to anyone – the prospect of spending rest of her life in prison was motivation enough for her to keep very, very quiet. It had to have been Conor who talked … how dare he betray her confidence like this; and then to have the audacity to lie to her about it.'

She shook her head in desperation and slugged back the rest of her glass of brandy, grimacing.

* * * *

Walking along one of the jetties at the marina, between the rows upon rows of high masts, that towered tall, as though piercing the cloudless sky, Conor stopped still. Hands in his pockets, he looked past the abundance of luxurious, sailing boats, out into the gently, lapping waters beyond and sighed. He couldn't believe that Lisa had accused him of divulging her secret to Riana. Why would he disclose something so important; so private? Why didn't she trust him?

He gritted his teeth in anger.

Chapter 40

Pulling a brush through her silky hair, Riana Beaumont stood in front of one of the dressing mirrors in her Dover based boutique, flicking and ruffling her fringe with her fingers. "Quiet this morning, isn't it?" she began as Jo dashed around behind her, at high speed, polishing counter tops and wiping door handles. "Quiet yes. Quiet... but its always quiet at this time of morning... We have two fittings booked for this afternoon as it is", she said, as she stopped to look crossly at a stubborn mark on one of the rectangular, brass, hand-plates on the stock room door.

Riana whirled around and brushed down her fire-engine red, military style, three quarter length coat. "I have a lunch time appointment myself... Will you manage the fittings alone Jo?" she asked.

Jo began rubbing vigorously at the smudge. "I've managed the last six months on my own haven't I?" she said bluntly, without turning. Riana smiled. She knew that Jo was a little riled about being abandoned again today, after her only having just returned from London - but she was the boss after all. What good is being the boss if you can't take liberties every once and a while? Anyway, she also knew that, deep-down Jo was delighted to have attained so much responsibility since the opening of the second shop in London. "You've done a great job here Jo" she remarked as she went to pick up her handbag, smirking, as she glimpsed the reflection of Jo's beaming face in the, now shining, brass, hand plate.

As she approached the front door, the bell jingled loudly and it opened towards her.

It took her a moment, but then recognition appeared on Riana's face. "Lisa… hi how are you?" she asked. Lisa breezed in past her – the scent of Chanel no. 5 wafting after her. She was wearing a luxurious, cream, mohair jumper, pulled in at the waist by a gorgeous, diamante stud belt; she wore a pair of fitted, skinny-leg jeans, and had teamed the outfit, with a stunning pair of sling-back, Minolo Blahniks. Her dark hair was swept back; her eyes highly defined by a smoky, dark eye shadow. She looked fantastic, powerful - but in actuality, she felt quite the opposite. Riana, however, was immediately impressed by this well dressed, compelling lady, and certainly in comparison to the tired, drawn looking woman she had met a few days before.

"Riana, is there somewhere we can talk…?" asked Lisa, "…in private?" she continued, as she eyed the peculiar little woman in the background.

"Absolutely" Riana replied, a little taken aback. She wondered why would Lisa be so interested in seeing her all of a sudden? She couldn't get rid of her fast enough the other day… it had to be something to do with Conor.

Riana turned on her heel and led the way, past a curious looking Jo, to the back of the shop. She tugged at a small handle, which opened a door, discreetly veiled behind a full-length mirror. They stepped inside and Lisa pulled the mirrored door shut behind her. They walked through a short corridor, lined at either side by clothes rails and large boxes, reaching at the end, a small room with a computer desk and filing cabinet at one side, and a kitchenette at the other; the whole place rather untidy, in an organised but chaotic fashion, a drastic difference to the immaculate boutique on the other side.

Riana walked to the kitchenette and gestured to Lisa, to sit at one of the two chairs. Lisa did as she was told. Riana flicked on the kettle. "Coffee?" she asked politely. Lisa nodded – wishing that Riana would be a little ruder or discourteous, so that she could

145

justify what she was about to accuse her of.

Riana sat down opposite Lisa and suddenly started talking; quickly; apologetically.

"Lisa, I offended you the other day, I know I did. I can come across as being a bit… snobbish… but it wasn't intentional…. Well, okay, maybe it was - a little - but… I hadn't seen Conor in six months and… oh look, I sensed your jealousy and I immediately played on it… I don't even know why I did it. Lisa I love Conor to bits, but I've moved on from him now… I don't want him back…He clearly wants you though"

Riana was being very honest with her. Lisa looked to the table, a distinct sense of shame welling up inside her. Perhaps she had been wrong about Riana… or else this was all a cunning plan to divert her attention. Riana got up and made the coffee. Still, Lisa was quiet.

Eventually, when Riana was seated once again and was pushing the milk and sugar across the table, Lisa finally regained her courage and spoke.

"Riana, I was a bit offended but …that's not what this is about. The other night when you and Conor went for drinks together… he told you something. Something he should never have mentioned… and you think you can use it but you don't realise the seriousness of all of this. I know that you know what I'm talking about - so you can drop the pretence".

Riana's face didn't react as Lisa expected. Her brow creased; confusion rested on her fine features. Lisa sighed. "Come on… at least admit it to me" she continued, a little desperately. Riana took a sip of her coffee and an awkward silence fell for a moment as Lisa waited for some form of a response.

"Look Lisa," Riana began finally; Lisa leaned forward, ready for the truth. " …I really have no idea what on earth you are talking about. If I did, I promise you I would tell you… now if Conor has told me anything, it's only how fond he is of you. He talked about you for most of the night – in fact, trying to get a word in edgeways was the only problem - and that's not a problem I normally encounter" she finished with a smirk. Lisa was shocked. She could virtually see the sincerity in Riana's eyes and realised, with a jolt, that she was wrong, very wrong.

She looked to the table. Suddenly she wished that the ground would open up and swallow her; maybe she could clamber in behind those cardboard boxes and stay hiding in that secret, mirrored, corridor forever. Silence fell again, while Lisa rapidly tried to think how she might remedy the situation.

Riana felt concern for this, clearly troubled, lady. "Is there something I can help you with Lisa?" asked Riana kindly. "If there is, I will …gladly. Any friend…girlfriend… of Conors is a friend of mine", she added.

Lisa stood up. Her hands were shaking. "I'm sorry Riana. I shouldn't have jumped to conclusions about you… or about Conor. I must have been mistaken. I'll go"

Riana stood up also, reaching forward and grabbing Lisa by the arm. "Lisa, please, if there is something troubling you…"

Lisa interjected quickly. "I can't tell you Riana. I'm sorry. I wish I could".

With that, she walked away, through the mirrored door, past a bemused Jo, and left the shop.

Riana shook her head, perplexed.

Chapter 41

Leaving lunchtimes' few straggling punters behind her, 19 year old, Sasha King thrust aside her apron, donned her light jacket and walked out from the pubs dingy darkness into the late afternoon's glow. As she strolled past the shops towards the Town Hall, she noticed a familiar figure walking in her direction. The curvaceous individual strutted towards her and as she recognised who it was, Sasha immediately felt herself redden. "Hi Lisa" she began nervously.

"Hi Sasha. Finished your shift for today then?" asked Lisa with feigned interest; too much on her mind to genuinely care.

"Yeah… just heading home… are you off to the pub?"

"No, I'm heading home now too".

Sasha smiled awkwardly. After a few seconds of discomfited silence, she suddenly gestured a hasty goodbye and moved off. Lisa watched the red-faced young woman and frowned. 'That was strange' she thought. 'She looked…almost guilty… like she knew something…'

Lisa began to walk away, and then suddenly she whirled around and called out "Sasha… wait up"

Sasha looked back… she slowed to a hesitant stop and waited tentatively as Lisa caught up with her. "You know don't you?" Lisa asked, as she approached, a little breathless.

Sasha looked to the ground; growing shame evident in her eyes. "I'm sorry Lisa…".

I promised myself that I wouldn't say anything but then I thought he had a right to know and …" she looked distraught. "I'm so sorry… God knows who I've gone and upset".

Lisa was silent. She was upset and confused.

"Sasha, who did you tell? What exactly did you say?"

Sasha looked at her feet. "Look I'm sorry… but I don't want to be involved in any of this".

With that, the agitated and flustered looking youngster took off power walking down the nearest side street.

At this stage, Lisa was baffled but at least things were beginning to make a little more sense now. Sasha had obviously overheard Lisa telling Conor in the pub that night. But then there was the question of who had Sasha told? She didn't believe for one second that the timid, sweet, Sasha had sent that note. Then a thought occurred to her.

Had Sharon received one too?

Rushing to her car, she jumped in and the engine started with a roar as she accelerated down the street to head back to the cottages.

The door to Sharon's cottage was open, as was the boot of her car. As Lisa pulled up, she saw Sharon struggling out the door with a large flat package, wrapped in brown paper.

Lisa got out of her car and marched across to the driveway. "Hi Lisa" said Sharon as she placed the package into the boot. "Just another painting I think Jacques will be interested in"… She looked up, wiping her brow. "I'm going back to Calais this evening. Going to spend a week there this time…"

"Sharon we need to talk…"

Sharon sighed. "Lisa… If we are ever going to get over this thing, then we have got to stop talking it to death".

"Well maybe you're right…. but this needs to be said" she moved closer to Sharon and lowered her voice. "I got a note"

"What kind of a note?"

"A one-liner … It said '*Your secret's out*'. Did you get one too?"

Sharon slammed the boot down. She looked both surprised and ill all at once. "No, no I didn't get one… who has he gone and told?" she snapped angrily, referring of course to Conor.

"I don't think he did… I mean… I accused him of telling Riana… but now I think that the barmaid at 'The Port Hole' might have overheard me telling him, and then she blabbed to someone else…. Only I don't know who…and" she gasped for breath before continuing, "…and now I've pissed off Conor and accused Riana in the wrong, and I'm still none the wiser. And why didn't you get one? Does this person think that I'm the one who killed Bryan?"

"Ssshh" whispered Sharon as she looked around her cautiously. "The barmaid knows? Bloody Hell Lisa, this is out of control… let's go over to yours and talk this through", she suggested, panic evident now in her wavering voice.

Lisa nodded.

As the neared the house, Lisa pulled out her keys and was just about to put them in the lock, when her eyes fell upon something sticking out from her letterbox. It was another brown envelope.

Sitting down now, inside the coolness of the cottage, Lisa felt utterly baffled and rather overcome with emotion. "What is going on?" she asked despairingly, as Sharon ripped open the envelope. Sharon's eyes scanned the paper before looking disbelievingly, up at Lisa. "Well, …what is it?" Lisa demanded.

"It's … it's a blackmail threat….", stammered Sharon.

"Blackmail? Oh good God. What does it say?"

"Its says '*Lisa, …£50,000 by the end of the week, or it gets out…I'll be in touch.*'"

She showed the note to Lisa who took it with trembling fingers. She sighed and a flood of tears accompanied her distressed expression as she read the scrawled note. She was exhausted from this entire nightmare.

"They know you have money – and I that I don't, I guess", said

Sharon under her breath as she sat opposite a disillusioned Lisa.

"What will we do? They have us over a barrel. They know we can't rightly bring the letters to the police" cried Lisa.

"Well… I don't have fifty grand" began Sharon. "…So, maybe its time we did what they least expect us to. Maybe its time we did go to the police with this whole mess… like we should have from the beginning".

"What? Oh great – *now* you want to do the right thing" said Lisa disbelievingly "Well" she continued, "we sure as hell can't do that now… they will want to know why the notes came to me and not you… they will know that I knew all along…they might even think that I killed him"

Sharon nodded. "You're right. Well, then …we have to pay them the money and hope we can stop it at that… can you get your hands on £50,000?" asked Sharon.

Lisa put her head in her hands. "Yes of course - if I have to", she said through her palms.

Sharon looked anxiously at Lisa. "Lisa…. If you can get hold of the cash, then I suggest we pay it… it will buy us both some more time… at least until we can find out who this leech is". Lisa nodded, inadvertently tasting her own tears as they rolled relentlessly down her cheeks.

Chapter 42

That evening, Lisa swapped her glittering, Minolo Blahniks, for a pair of hiking boots, which, needless to say, looked slightly absurd, when teamed with the rest of her lovely attire. However, desperately needing space to think, she scrambled on up the grassy route, to the right of her cottage, until she reached a flat patch of ground at the front of the Western Heights, majestically overlooking the Harbour below.

She couldn't help but wonder, how one could manage to get enmeshed in something so ugly, in a place that managed to combine such activity, beauty and serenity?

She inhaled the fresh sea air deeply and closed her eyes. What was she going to do? She had four days to make a decision. Coming by the cash was not a problem, by any means; but everything else about the situation in which she found herself including having become the victim of a 'blackmail plot', was a big problem ... and one that was swiftly spiralling out of control.

She thought about home; about Sheila and Caroline; about her father and her mother; about Ben. Running back to London at this stage was definitely tempting, even despite the lengthy explanations she might have to offer, but it was clearly not going to help.

As she turned back and looked to the vastness of the ocean before her, she decided that she needed a break – space to make a decision about what to do next. She groaned at how ironic it sounded, as essentially, she was looking for a 'break' from her so-called 'break'. However, with only until the end of the week to contemplate what to do, she finally decided that she would head for Calais to join

Sharon.

Perhaps, under the circumstances, Sharon was the last person she should be spending time with, but she was also, at the moment, a kindred spirit, of sorts; united by a common bond, however disturbing that bond might be.

She smiled softly - 'yes a few days in the historic haven and shopping paradise of Calais, was just what the doctor ordered'.

Clambering back down the incline, she reached the edge of the path just in time to see Sharon's car head off, down over the next hill. She waved wildly at it but despite her frantic beckoning, she watched, disappointed, as its' tail lights' blinked red, and disappeared from view.

'Never mind', she thought, she would try and book a space on the Hoverspeed Catamaran, first thing.

* * * *

The windscreen wipers swished back and forth, as Lisa sat patiently in her car.

The weather was truly unpredictable of late; the previous days sun had, once again, changed overnight to being misty and drizzly. One by one, the line of cars boarded the ferry.

After a while, Lisa found the familiar, gentle, movement of the Catamaran on the ocean, and the hum of its large engines, to be positively soothing.

As she looked around her, everyone appeared to have left their vehicles, except for a gentleman three cars to her right who was catching some shuteye, and Lisa herself, who was using the time to think. She hadn't really considered this trip very carefully. Having bunged some clothes in a case and bought a three-day, open / return ticket, here she was, heading to France, without a place to stay, or indeed having any idea of where Sharon was likely to be – and with Sharon's mobile seemingly switched off, finding her, was suddenly going to prove harder than she had hoped.

153

She remembered the name of the art dealer that Sharon had mentioned. 'Jacques Dupont' …and although did not know where his gallery was, Lisa decided that it most likely, wouldn't be too hard to find.

At worst, she wouldn't find Sharon at all, but at least she would have some time to herself in another very inspiring part of the world; what used to be known to the French as the 'pays reconquis' or re-conquered territory – after being liberated from English reign by French forces in the sixteenth century but only then, to get a rather rough deal some time later, in both the following twentieth-century wars. She mused over what little she knew of Calais' history before then turning her thoughts to her writing project - the fictional tale 'Black Wednesday' – realising, with some dismay, how much of a back seat it had taken over the past couple of weeks.

Suddenly, after what felt like only moments, folk began to return to their vehicles. Some had merely wandered around the ferry, some had remained in the cafes upstairs and others had spent the short trip clinging happily to the railings on deck, returning now to their cars and vans with windswept hair and spray-soaked faces.

Lisa sat up and clicked back on her seat belt; preparing to alight on French soil.

Despite her family's wealth, and many foreign breaks over the years, she had never been to Northern France before. She had, of course, visited Paris, which was some 148 miles south of Calais, on many separate occasions. Her most memorable trip to Paris was her very first visit and was the one when, late one summers evening, Ben had carefully proposed to her on the banks of the Seine, underneath a prettily-pruned, ever-green, dotted with tiny, white, fairy lights – and she sighed as she remembered how excited she had been; if only she had been able to foresee the years of loneliness that lay ahead, she may not have been so quick to say 'yes'.

They began to descend from the ferry via a series of raised roads and she found herself weaving, through the hectic port and along the route in towards the town centre of Calais.

The built up waterfront greeted her with its apartment style buildings and traffic filled streets. She smiled at the hustle and bustle. It wasn't raining and certainly wasn't as overcast a morning as what she had left behind her in Dover, not even an hour earlier. Folk were walking around in t-shirts and shorts, despite the slight sense of coolness in the air.

With one of the biggest shopping centres in Europe, Calais was now one of the foremost destinations for British shoppers. Hundreds of British day-trippers poured into Calais that day. The ferry companies were very busy and Lisa was rather lucky to have managed to get a ticket that morning.

As the morning went on, Lisa was very impressed by its town centre, which housed a huge sample of independent, family run businesses as well as large shopping centres, clothes boutiques and supermarkets.

When it was under British reign, Calais was sometimes refereed to as 'The brightest jewel in the English crown' because of its importance as the ultimate 'gateway' to Europe. Apart from its' obviously significant location, Lisa could really see why people were so taken with the town; she found it wonderfully quaint as well as being clearly progressive, and could definitely see herself falling, very much, in love with Calais. Queen Mary I of England was reported as having said "when I am dead and opened, you shall find Calais lying in my heart". Lisa smiled as she considered how rapidly it was finding a place in her heart too.

She strolled through a vibrant and intriguing country-style, market in Place d'Armes; sampling fresh foods, chocolates, patisseries and cheeses; only finally leaving, with her tummy full of rich morsels, …and before she might, shamefully, have to sneak open the top button of her pants.

After that she decided to seat herself down at an outdoor café. Sharon's phone was still switched off. A little unsure of herself, she sat sipping cappuccino, smoking a cigarette and silently marvelling at the famous Rodin sculpture of the 'Six Burghers of Calais' in front of the Town Hall, just visible in the distance. She sketchily recalled what she had once read about those courageous men. … How British forces had trapped the inhabitants of Calais within the walls of their own town during a siege that lasted eleven months; the people of Calais were all starving and six brave men offered their lives in return for the rest of the townsfolk being spared. Edward III agreed to this and was about to kill the men, but for his queen took pity on the brave six and agreed to spare their lives, …but only if the town surrendered to the British in return. Lisa looked now across at the statue of the six men and flushed, as she considered the situation both herself and Sharon were in. Those men were honourable, decent folk. She certainly didn't feel honourable or decent right now. Those men, despite having lost their town for the best part of two centuries, were still national heroes in Calais. They had put their principals aside, and had placed the good of the townsfolk ahead of themselves – in the end, being rewarded with their lives.

Sharon should have put her selfish principles aside; placing morality and decency to the fore… Doing the 'right thing' should have come first for Sharon and for Lisa - and perhaps it would then have had its own reward…

"Its marvellous isn't it?" came a distinctly French accent from alongside her, interrupting her thoughts.

She whirled around. A suited gentleman sat at the very next table from her. He had been watching closely, as she stared across at the statue. "Yes" she replied. "Its inspirational". He smirked at her obvious London accent and she blushed a little.

"Are you on holidays?" he enquired.

"Yeah… a short break" she replied a little coyly.

He nodded. "Very nice"

Suddenly, deciding to seize the opportunity, she leaned forward a little, and continued to ask the gentleman "I don't suppose you could tell me where I might find an art gallery owned by a man called Jacques Dupont?" she asked hopefully.

The man smiled cordially. "Yes of course". He pointed to the streets behind them. "The street adjacent to this one… you must first pass the police station, and at the very end is 'Dupont's Galerie'. It is upstairs, above the petite boulangerie, with the rouge canopy". She grinned. "Merci" she replied. She stubbed her cigarette in the tiny ashtray and stood to leave. He stood also, reaching forward and taking her hand in his, before bringing it to his lips. His moustache tickled her skin and she felt herself flush once again. Grabbing her clutch bag from the table, she smiled at the man. "Au-revoir" she said quickly, and left.

Chapter 43

Walking up the three, weathered, stone steps to a shop entrance, Lisa stopped for a moment under a large, red, awning with the word 'Boulangerie' written across it. She inhaled the enticing aroma of freshly baked baguettes and patisseries, which wafted from the open window, before looking around her. A second door could be seen to the right of the bakery. The gold, somewhat uneven, block lettering, printed on the glass read 'Galerie Dupont'.

Inside, she climbed some steep, carpeted stairs, which ended at a tiny, threadbare landing. Directly to the left of the landing, there was a pokey little window overlooking the busy street below, and a further door. On pushing open this door, it was like 'leaving the courtyard and entering the palace'. The calming fragrance of lavender fused with what she thought smelt like vanilla, immediately drifted towards her; a middle-aged lady, dripping with jewellery and beautifully dressed in a cream trouser suit, was standing behind a pedestal-like, reception desk, browsing through some pamphlets.

She smiled broadly, speaking to Lisa, in prompt, welcoming French. Lisa shrugged her shoulders "I'm sorry, I don't speak much French", she said regretfully. She had, of course, like most of her teenage counterparts, studied French throughout school, but, somewhat to her own dismay, she had carried very little of it through to her adult life. It had certainly proved a handicap over the years, though to her relief, most of the locals she had encountered today were indeed very articulate when it came to conversing in English.

This woman was, thankfully, no different. She nodded understandingly. "That is fine Mademoiselle".... "Can I be of any assistance?"

Lisa smiled appreciatively. "Thanks but is it okay if I just look around?"

The woman nodded courteously, her soft auburn hair, glinting under the sun that sneaked in from a tiny skylight above her head. "Of course" she smiled, before then returning her concentration and her ring-clad fingers to the pamphlets on her desk.

Lisa continued to saunter around the charming gallery. Its' honey-cream walls were dotted with paintings. Plinths stood here and there, sat upon by interesting wooden carvings and many beautiful, bronze sculptures. The background music was low and relaxing. Despite her mounting worries, Lisa felt curiously at ease in the gallery's calm surroundings.

Meandering along, gazing admiringly from one painting to another, she finally spotted, in the farthest corner, a series of four pictures, side by side, which she thought she vaguely recognised. On closer examination of the first picture, Lisa confirmed to herself that it was positively one of Bryans' pieces. She remembered having seen it hanging, compellingly, in the Wilks' sitting room, in pride of place, over their mantle. It was a scene from Dover entitled 'The Citadel'- Its' old ruins, beautifully depicted, in muted colours and fine lines. On the bottom right hand corner of the picture, were the initials 'BW' in neat black handwriting.

She looked with interest to the others.

The second portrait was entitled 'The Majestic Whites', depicting an image of Dover's famous White Cliffs; the next was of 'Dover Castle', not quite as striking but enchanting nonetheless and the final picture portrayed the impressive opening of the 'Grand Shaft' with an enticing, glimpse of the striking horizon view in the background. All four pictures bore the same distinctive style, and indeed the same initials.

At that moment, a small, white card caught her eye; positioned

159

underneath the paintings, it contained four lines of fine print. Leaning forward, she noticed that the first two lines were in French, the second two, in English.

She read the latter two lines.
Title: 'Scenes of Dover' series – Artist: Bernard Witherspoon. Items can be purchased separately.
She looked at the name on the card, and then to the pictures.
'BW'? … 'Bernard Witherspoon'?
That was peculiar. She had definitely identified the signature and recognised at least one, if not two of the paintings, to be Bryans. Perhaps Sharon had decided to sell the paintings under an assumed name? Well, considering the furore surrounding his death she decided that, perhaps, that was acceptable enough.

She looked back up at the pictures.

They were spectacular; his attention to detail was remarkable. Definitely, the most striking of them all was the final one, 'The Grand Shaft'; the exquisite fusion of summer flowers peppered throughout the long, billowing, green grass; the starkness of the dark tunnel, or what little could be seen of it from that interesting angle, and the depth of the blue sky in the background, …it was captivating…

Then suddenly, as her eyes continued to wander over the many little bumps of colour on the canvas, she saw something… something that made her cheeks flush and her heartbeat quicken. Immediately, she straightened up, trying to catch both her breath and her thoughts.

Deliberating for a brief moment, she then hurriedly returned her gaze to the picture; staring intently at it once again…

'That can't be' she thought… 'It's just not possible'.

"Is everything alright Mademoiselle?"

Startled, she turned around. A man was standing directly behind her, smiling amiably. He was informally attired, with a kerchief-style necktie, which she thought to be stereotypical of a French artistic type, but otherwise his clothes were rather streamlined and expensive. He definitely had a palpable air of wealth about him. Was he, in fact, very successful? She had never heard of him, however, she was admittedly ignorant in matters of any artistic significance and so she quickly disregarded her attempted analysis of this handsome young gentleman. "Are you Jacques Dupont?" she asked, her voice wavering slightly.

His smile broadened. "Oui… that is me"

"Mr. Dupont…" she continued, thinking how approachable he seemed. "A friend of mine sold you these paintings. Sharon Wilks… I was supposed to meet her today but her phone is switched off… I'm afraid I can't get hold of her. Is she coming back this evening by any chance?"

He shook his head, pouting his bottom lip in an exaggerated expression of regret. "Non … I am sorry - but I do not think she will be returning today. I was waiting for a painting from this series" he said, pointing to the paintings, "…and she brought it to me this morning… along with one other piece that I requested" he gestured to a further picture in the far corner of the gallery, 'which must have been the one Sharon had struggled to put into her car the day before', Lisa thought to herself.

"…I have not seen her since she dropped them off, around eleven" he finished.

"Was this the one you were waiting for?" she asked, motioning towards 'The Grand Shaft'.

He nodded. "Oui …It is the last in the series. Very lovely isn't it? I think I am becoming quite a fan of Monsieur Witherspoon's work…"

Lisa agreed nervously. "They are lovely pieces" she sighed. Looking awkwardly back to Mr Dupont, she smiled weakly, and suddenly felt the urge to leave "Actually… I really must go now…

but thank you Mr. Dupont".

As she turned to leave, Jacques Dupont tipped her on the shoulder. "I'm not sure if this will help at all …but Madame Wilks mentioned that she was staying at a hotel here in Calais. It is about fifteen minutes away …on the promenade…by the name of 'La Mer Libre'"

Lisa sighed in relief. "Thank you very much Mr Dupont… I really appreciate that".

Feeling an immediate rush of adrenalin, Lisa hastened out past two mystified browsers, and down the steep staircase. She skimmed the three stone steps, her feet barely touching the stone, and ran onto the street outside.

The sun was hiding now, having ducked in behind a thick band of cloud that had descended on the town. She stopped in the centre of the street, clutching her handbag in one hand, her keys in the other and gazed for a moment up into the gloomy skies.

Everything had just been turned, even further, upside down - but she was determined to confront Sharon… things weren't making any sense whatsoever now – and she just had to get to the bottom of it.

Chapter 44

Plush, glass swing-doors, adorned the wonderful stone façade of the old hotel, which loomed in front of her, as she stood now, feeling somewhat insignificant beneath its vast entrance. Most of the town of Calais had been firmly trampled beneath the wrath of the two twentieth century wars it had endured, so therefore very little of the original town still existed. However, this hotel, which was gloriously splendid looking, certainly appeared long-standing and Lisa wondered how old it was.

As she pondered this, a suitably attired, doorman smiled cordially and held open one of the shining glass doors. Lisa thanked him and entered into the airy foyer.

'La Mer Libre' or as it is translated, 'The Sea Room' was stunning, and its' décor truly coincided with its' given name. Sea-faring objects and artwork could be seen subtly positioned around the entire reception area. Throughout her life, Lisa was lucky enough to be extremely familiar with five-star opulence and she was duly impressed with this nautically inspired hotel. However if Sharon was, in fact, staying here, then, for someone who Lisa recently believed to be short of cash, she was certainly spending what little money she must have received from the paintings, very extravagantly.

At the hull-shaped, reception desk, a young man, most likely the concierge, spoke in rapid French to a lady on his left. She nodded and rushed off just as he turned to face Lisa.

"Hello…" she began, preparing to take a chance on this young man.

"Bonjour Mademoiselle…Can I help you?"

"I hope so… I'm looking for a friend of mine. The thing is …I don't actually have her room number. Could you give it to me?" she asked, knowing only too well that she was most likely 'flogging a dead horse'.

"Is your friend expecting you?" he asked politely.

"No… I would like it to be a surprise… is that possible? … Please?" she looked pleadingly at him.

However, the young concierge was already shaking his head. "I am very sorry mademoiselle… but I simply cannot give you a guests' room number unless the guest has approved it… It is our policy; Privacy reasons. What is their name? Perhaps if I ring them…"

Lisa interjected. "Oh no thanks… It's ok…" she replied. "I'll try her mobile phone again… thank you anyway".

The concierge nodded warmly at the pretty young woman; approvingly studying her curvy female form, as she strutted off towards the beautiful leather sofas in the lobby.

Sitting down, Lisa decided that ringing Sharon's mobile again, was indeed the only option left…

Opening her handbag, she picked out her phone and glanced up at the concierge who was still watching her. She smiled at him and held up the phone to show that she was indeed going to ring. He immediately returned her smile, a little embarrassed at having been caught staring, and hastily set about rustling the papers on his desk.

Lisa smirked.

She dialled the number… silence… and then a message – it was switched off.

As she launched into dialling the number a second time she glanced over at the sizeable fireplace to her left.

Large dried flowers peered out from an ornate vase, aptly hiding the starkness of an empty grate, and a very substantial rectangular mirror hung grandly over it.

As she was listening to the recorded voice on the phone, and was contemplating leaving a message of some sort, she happened to spy, in the reflection of the mirror, a head of curly, red hair that she immediately recognised to be Sharon's.

Quickly, she huddled down, out of view, behind the oversized leather arm of the sofa and waited for Sharon to pass and start heading for the lift. Situated only a couple of feet from where Lisa was cowering, Sharon stepped inside the spacious, wood-panelled lift, and Lisa strained to hear her ask the young lift-attendant for the third floor, before the doors slid shut and the lift proceeded to whir upwards.

Lisa hastily jumped up and clutching her belongings, she rushed to the staircase.

She clambered, as fast as she could, which was proving awkward in her high heeled boots, up the six diagonal flights of marble steps; every second one stopping on a landing which opened into corridors of bedrooms. The third-floor door opened out, as did the others, at the far end of a long corridor. Hiding now in the shadows, she had no sooner arrived, panting, out of breath and mentally cursing her fitness – or lack of it - when she heard the familiar ping of the lift doors opening, half way down the corridor.

She watched carefully as Sharon marched out and strode to the door marked, in gold, by the number 311. Pushing a plastic card into the horizontal lock, the door clicked open and she disappeared inside.

This was Lisa's cue. She raced down on the soft and thick, burgundy-carpeted hallway and stood now opposite the room door. She took a deep breath.

This was it… Sharon had some very serious explaining to do… She held her hand up to knock on the door… but as she was about to let her fist fall on the dark wood, the door suddenly re-opened abruptly in front her.

Bryan Wilks was glaring back at her from over his wire-rim glasses.

Chapter 45

The hairs on the nape of her neck stood on end, sending a prickly and terrifying sensation down along her spine. She stood, open-mouthed, somewhat fearful and in total shock.

"I... I knew it", she stammered.

Bryan's face had drained of colour on having laid eyes on the surprised Londoner. "Lisa... what are you doing here? ...We can explain" he started nervously.

Lisa ignored him, and with a rush of courage, she pushed roughly in past the dazed Bryan.

On hearing a toilet flush as she entered, she spun around to see Sharon come strolling obliviously from the bathroom; though she stopped dead in her tracks on sight of Lisa, standing there in the middle of her hotel room.

"Oh Good God..." she started.

Lisa laughed affectedly. "God wont help you now Sharon..."

"Lisa... now don't panic... I can explain everything"

Bryan was about to open his mouth until a frantic Sharon glowered at him. He looked to the floor instead.

Lisa was gazing around her at the elaborate bedroom, tears glistening in her eyes as the enormity of the situation began to descend slowly on her bewildered brain.

"I saw your paintings today Bryan..." she began "I saw them ...and as I was looking at the last one... it dawned on me... that you had to be alive".

Bryan looked confused.

Sharon stepped forward. "What do you mean?" she asked. Lisa

turned to Sharon. "Your plan wasn't as fool proof as you thought was it?" she said snidely. Sharon cocked her head sideways. "Now Lisa, this wasn't about hurting you"

Lisa completely ignored Sharon's dismal attempt at appeasing the situation, cutting roughly across her and turning back to a baffled Bryan.

"It was your attention to detail that let you down…" she continued "Your painting of 'The Grand Shaft'? … Oh it was gorgeous by the way, and it included every little feature… even down to the old broken signpost at the Shafts entrance; the signpost that *my friends and I* accidentally broke …like four days *after* your alleged death".

She turned back to Sharon; looking despairingly at her…. feeling very hurt.

"It took me a few minutes for it to make any kind of sense… and even when it did, it still didn't… The first thing that came into my head was that you must have painted it yourself, with Bryan so clearly being dead… but yet I knew you wouldn't have achieved anything near as fine. That's when I realised that the only other conclusion was that Bryan couldn't possibly be dead. …I guess you simply took a photo of the Grand Shaft, and brought it out here last week… once you knew the gallery were interested in a fourth".

Sharon sat on the edge of the large four-poster bed. "Yes… that's right" she sighed.

Lisa looked angrily at the suddenly rather morose, Sharon.

"Why… Sharon? How could you do all this to me? How could you put me through this hell? *Why* would you put me through this hell?"

Sharon put her hands to her face and groaned loudly; tears fell as she turned her face to look back up at Lisa through bleary eyes.

But Lisa wasn't affected by this exhibition of contrived sorrow and remorse; she had seen Sharon in action, feigning grief at the cliffs edge, at the funeral and indeed throughout the entire ordeal. She had fooled everyone… most of all, Lisa.

"Save the bogus tears Sharon, I've seen it all before" she said crossly.

Sharon continued to try. "Lisa I'm so sorry. I didn't mean to take you for a ride but…" she stopped as Lisa abruptly cut across her once again.

"The night you called around…" she started, walking around now, looking vaguely, speaking quickly, as though she were trying to piece together all the sinister twists to this tale. "… Your hands were covered in blood. Obviously that wasn't real… but you said that you had killed him… you were so genuine. You were in pieces… I really thought you'd done it… seeing as how he'd been hitting you …and the bruises…" she paused, as even more, sick realisation appeared on her face.

"The bruises… they were for my benefit too weren't they?" she asked quietly.

Silence…

"*Weren't they?*" she shouted at Sharon.

"Yes!"…. Sharon retorted loudly. She paused and started to snivel. "Yes they were… I'm part of the drama society remember… bruises and blood are easy to fake when you have the right accessories".

"…Yeah and when you are a cold hearted bitch that doesn't care about anyone but herself" Lisa responded angrily; she shook her head in disgust. "And then the lies… the constant lies… the suicide was a fake regardless, but this… this just takes the biscuit. I went through mental hell to help keep your sordid secret and all along you were laughing behind my back? What was this all about Sharon? What was it for? My money?"

Sharon sniped back. "Yes it was about money Lisa… okay? Money!" She looked down at her feet and, suddenly she, somewhat shamefully, began to recount her odious plan. "…I knew the minute you moved into the cottage that you were independently rich. Bryan and I were in dire straights. He had run up some very serious debts and we couldn't meet them. He was beginning to get really depressed and …" she looked across at Bryan, who was sitting now in a wicker chair in the corner of the room; silent; his fingers in beneath his glasses, rubbing hard at his tired eyes. She continued "…And his work was suffering. We came up with the plot that if he were to 'supposedly' die, we could kiss goodbye to our debts, claim what meagre bit of insurance money we were entitled to and up sticks to France. I knew that getting him to Calais would be no problem… he left that very night by ferry. No one was searching for him at that stage, so his passport was barely checked. He immediately posted it back to me on arrival in Calais, so that a couple of days later, when the police looked for it, I was able to present it. The plan was he would stay in hiding in Calais until I had sorted everything in Dover. Then I would join him and we would start afresh - with him living under an assumed name… somewhere in the south of France or Spain perhaps… When you arrived at the cottage, you… you were like our meal ticket to an easier life, our chance to escape. I had to befriend you in order to make you believe me…to believe that I was being abused and was driven to killing my own husband because by knowing everything, you were somehow involved… Oh God above Lisa I am so sorry…"

Lisa was cold and indifferent, as she suddenly knew what was coming next.

"….And the blackmail threats? They were you too?"

Sharon nodded in shame. "You needed to think you were hiding something… something really serious… so that we could blackmail you. I knew you would tell someone. In fact, I was banking on you letting this secret slip, and as long as it wasn't to the police, then we were safe enough. With you thinking that someone had betrayed your confidence, then it was easy to blackmail you". Lisa listened on in stunned silence.

Sharon continued. "That fifty grand was going to help us disappear… I discovered that we weren't entitled to our insurance money because of some suicide clause we weren't aware of…"

"Fifty-grand though Sharon? Why didn't you blackmail me for more money? You could have…"

"I wasn't going to push you into the arms of the law by asking for too much money – besides, it was all we needed to disappear" she hesitated. "…I had grown so fond of you though… It wasn't easy for me Lisa… perhaps we were deluded, I don't know but please believe me when I say I am sorry".

Lisa looked on at Sharon with real disdain. "Not easy for you? For Christ's sake Sharon, if you had just asked me for some cash maybe I could have helped you out… But instead you do all of this - a string of structured lies. I will never believe another word that falls from your lying lips" Lisa's arms had begun waving wildly around her now in anger and disbelief. "…You aren't sorry" she went on. "Oh you might be feeling a bit sorry that you've been caught out… sorry that your big plan has been ruined… but you are not sorry for what you did to me…" tears flowed faster as she spoke "I was going bloody mad Sharon… losing sleep, feeling ill; I was constantly doubting myself and was so close to telling the police so many times… especially after the funeral service".

She suddenly whirled around to stare at Bryan. "Your mother Bryan…" she whispered sadly. "She was so broken… devastated. She spoke so devotedly of you at your *'service'*… and was so hurt that you had committed suicide. It made me violently ill to know… or to think I knew… that you had been murdered…and you could do that to her? What kind of person does that make you? Was your life really that bad?"

Bryan shook his head.

"*Mother*" he whispered to himself, clearly troubled. Lisa thought she spied a lone tear escape down his cheek, but she couldn't be sure. Disturbed, she turned back to Sharon.

"But I didn't go to the police Sharon, because I didn't want to let you down... As much as I hated myself for it, I had given you my word. I don't even know whether to believe any of this story of yours...but the difference is that now I don't care - I just don't care"

She started to approach Sharon and stood, bending down, close to her face, her hot, angry, breath, blowing the flyaway strands of hair from Sharon's brow.

"You are nothing more than a pathetic, lying, deceitful bitch... and I will never forgive you for this...ever!" she whispered forcefully. She stood up straight.

"*Your secret's out*" she said crossly, before turning on her heel and storming out.

Bryan, distressed, was about to stand up, but decided against it, slumping back into his chair and looking despairingly at his wife. Sharon jumped up and raced to the door. "Lisa.... What are you going to do? LISA?"

Sharon stood in the hallway, watching Lisa march off. She leaned wearily against the wall and cried.

She knew what Lisa would do... What she should have done all along.

Chapter 46

Sitting in her car, around the corner from the hotel, Lisa buried her head in her hands and cried… but after a few moments of unconscious lamentation, she began mulling over the entire elaborate hoax. It dawned on her that despite feeling appalled, disturbed and hurt, she was also feeling an overwhelming sense of relief. Relief that, apart from being quite clearly gullible, naïve, and whatever else she could label herself, she was, however, no longer privy to a murder …and even though Bryan and Sharon were both exposed to her as liars, she was incredibly thankful that he was still alive…and it appeared he was clearly more of a spineless idiot than a vicious, wife-beating thug. She was also relieved that Sharon wasn't a murderess – although the reality of her persona was not all that appealing either.

As she looked up at her snivelling, blubbering, reflection in the rear-view mirror, she thought of Conor. The gorgeous, gentle Conor…. and how she had wronged him; accused him of divulging her secret… accused him of desiring Riana… she hadn't known Conor very long, but she was so in love with him… yes, definitely in love with him.

A smile twitched at the ends of her mouth, as she contemplated getting back to Dover and telling him everything. She wiped her eyes and face with a tissue and turned the key… the engine started with a rumble and she began to laugh aloud as she took off through the pretty French port-town, in the direction of the ferry berths.

Chapter 47

Having managed to get back on to the late-evening crossing, Lisa stood now, like many others, grasping the cool, metal railings on deck, letting the rain dampen her skin, feeling the magnificent breeze sweep through her hair, the rich sea air filling her lungs and the weight, that she had been carrying around for the past few weeks, lift gradually from her shoulders and float away across the heaving waves, that rose and fell ahead of the large boat.

She contemplated her situation and decided that telling the police was the next logical step, …and that it might not end up being too daunting a situation, as she merely wouldn't implicate herself. She would without a doubt, play the innocent card, concluding that 'as far as she was aware', Bryan Wilks had committed suicide… until she bumped into him in Calais and it was there and then that Sharon had told her everything. She would conveniently omit any details regarding bruises, handguns, tall-tales of murder and blackmail threats. If Sharon decided to try and put Lisa in the frame, then, to any sensible ear, it would sound utterly ridiculous… and besides, she suddenly felt confident that Sharon wouldn't implicate her at all. Why? Because she believed that, despite herself, Sharon had grown fonder of Lisa than she had ever originally intended.

As the ferry approached land, glimpses of a crimson and orange sunset filtered its way through the gentle rain and the gathering clouds, reflecting iridescently on the lapping waters. Lisa returned quickly to her car, blowing into her hands to warm them up; she was waiting eagerly to disembark in Dover, and locate Conor. Perhaps the Kent Police should have been her first stop, but she was following her aching heart now, not her head.

She knew that Conor should be working, so she would be heading straight to the Cargo Terminal.

Her heart began to race as she drove along the busy waterfront. She couldn't wait to see him again, to smell him again and to be hugged by him again. It was as though she hadn't seen him for weeks and yet, she had only known him as long.

She desperately hoped that he would forgive her for being so quick to jump to the wrong conclusions …doubting his intentions with Riana, and doubting his loyalty to her.

Pulling into the yard at the Cargo Terminal, Lisa parked her car near the entrance and got out, her heels clicking loudly on the concrete as she upped the pace, eager to find Conor.

She looked all around her… the rain that had fallen ever so gently during the crossing, now had started to fall much harder, so she couldn't see very far ahead. Forklifts whirred around her and men walked too and fro in huge waterproof coats.

As she neared one of the huge cargo containers, she stopped dead in her tracks.

There, under shelter from an old tarpaulin, stood Conor   … but with his arms draped around Riana Beaumont.

He was embracing her; lifting her high, so that her feet were raised off the ground, arched behind her …and she was squealing in excitement.

Lisa's stomach churned and she felt instantly ill.

But he said he didn't want her… she said she didn't want him. They lied… why would he lie to her? Why was everyone suddenly lying to her?

Conor had just carefully planted a kiss, firmly on Riana's cheek when he glanced to his right and caught sight of Lisa, standing there, like a drowned rat; her hair clinging to her face, her expression full of shock and hurt. Suddenly, she turned around and started to walk quickly in the opposite direction.

"LISA" he called after her. She ignored him.

Sensing that he had started to follow … she walked a little faster, and then began to run… awkwardly, in the lashing rain. Why was he bothering to follow? What was he going to say? It all seemed very clear to Lisa. It didn't need any explanations as far as she was concerned.

She was gutted. Her heart felt as though, all in one day, it had been danced and trampled upon by the two people she had been gullible enough to have faith in during her time in Dover. There was no excuse other than she must be a very naïve and clearly, very foolish woman, and she was suddenly more determined than ever, to pack her bags and return to the life she had left behind… perhaps it wasn't perfect, but with all its flaws, she had never felt so daft, or so unbelievably hurt, when she was living at home in London.

Conor took off running now to catch up with her.

Having reached the car at this stage, Lisa pressed the button on her key; the lights blinked twice and with a customary bleeping noise, the car was open. She reached out to grab the door but suddenly Conor was at her side, his hand grabbing her wrist and whirling her around to face him.

He stood close to her, very close; his breath on her face, his deep blue eyes studying her expression – and they both were quiet for a moment. The rain was soaking them; running down their faces, clinging to his strong features; mingling with Lisa's warm tears.

"Lisa…" he began finally. "It's absolutely not what you think". He was whispering gently, stroking away wet strands of hair from her face.

She shook him free. "Of course it is…do you think I'm blind?"

He looked hurt. "Well yeah actually…. Blind enough that you

didn't see Riana's fiancé standing two feet away from us" he said gently, but earnestly.

Lisa faltered. "W…What?"

She was confused.

"Riana just got engaged to a man she's been seeing in London. Bit of a whirlwind romance; they only met about five weeks ago… like you and me. They are in love and she just told me the news… Lisa, I was congratulating her".

Lisa groaned inwardly. That's why they were hugging. She flushed furiously.

"I'm sorry…" she began, hanging her head to hide her shame. He smirked and stroked her face again, pushing her chin up to face him. "You don't have to be…" he replied.

"Yes I do…but for more than you think. I should never have accused you of telling Riana about … well, you know. I should never have doubted you, not even for a second.

"I understand you doubting me at first… but I thought you'd have believed me when I denied it… I wouldn't have done that to you" he said.

"I know that now"

"Do you?"

She nodded. "Yeah I do… I know almost too bloody much now…"

"Why? What's happened?" he asked, concerned.

She sighed. "Its Bryan Wilks. He wasn't murdered after all… he was never even dead… It was all a hoax …to blackmail me".

Conor listened on in bewildered silence as she recounted, briefly, what had happened since she last saw him. His jaw dropped as she related the ins and outs of Sharon's obnoxious plan. "So he's actually alive then? And all the guilt, and the heartache and the lies … they were the result of a bloody lie to begin with? … Lisa that's good news I suppose but you must be just knackered from this whole thing…" he said sympathetically.

She sniffed… wiping her nose and her teary face on the long bell sleeve of her jacket. Suddenly she started to giggle. Within seconds, her giggles had turned to outright laughter. He began to laugh too… "Why are we laughing?" he asked her through the rain. "Because it's all so ridiculous… and here we are, standing in the rain, getting absolutely soaked to the skin, and I must look such a mess…" she paused. "…And I love you"

He stopped laughing.

"I love you too" he replied.

…And they kissed.

Chapter 48

With happy hearts, they clung tightly to one another's sodden clothes, cuddling and squeezing as though afraid of ever letting go. However, after a few more moments of being semi-oblivious to the rain, they finally decided, sensibly, to take cover and they sat into Lisa's car, sinking into the soft leather seats and flicking on the heating.

It wasn't cold per se, as the temperatures had barely dropped during this heavy summer shower, but having become so saturated, Lisa was now shivering uncontrollably. "Are you okay? Come on you need to warm up" said Conor, concerned.

"I'm fine", she laughed, feeling as though she could freeze now for all she cared, as her nightmare was finally coming to an end. "Lets have a drink to celebrate", she suggested, as she rubbed her hands together for warmth.

"Right... but..." Conor was hesitating.

"Oh my good God..." gasped Lisa, as it dawned on her, the extent of the fuss she had just created in front of Riana and her fiancé. "I forgot all about Riana... you'd better go and find her" she said embarrassed.

"Well, actually, they left... Riana knew you would understand once I'd explained so they ran to their car to get out of the rain"

"Well please just ring her then Conor. God knows what she must think of me... especially after the whole shop incident"

"What shop incident?" Conor asked curiously.

"Oh, it was nothing really" replied Lisa, looking away. "I just don't want her to think I'm that shallow and silly...ask them to join us for a drink right now and I can apologise properly"

"Ok" he decided with a smile… "But I have to let Joe know that I'm heading off. …I'll be five minutes" he kissed her on the cheek and she watched him fondly as he darted back through the yard in the rain.

Sighing, she picked up her mobile phone, dialled a number and waited.

A female voice answered "Kent Police.…"

Lisa inhaled deeply. "Inspector Darren White please" she said, self-assuredly.

* * * *

Letting the intense steam from her hot-port, fused with the bitter spiciness of lemon and cloves, permeate all the nooks and crannies of her shivering frame, Lisa sat at the bar counter in 'The Port-Hole', contemplating her brief conversation with Inspector White. She was waiting for Conor to return from outside the pub, where he had been walking up and down on the path, talking on his mobile phone to Riana.

She looked up at him anxiously when he returned.

"Relax. She totally understood… she'll be here soon" he smiled.

"And her fiancé too?" asked Lisa.

"Yep… he didn't know what was going on when I ran off… he couldn't see you from where he was stood… and didn't know what I was up to. Poor guy…he was a bit confused"

Lisa smiled. "So he didn't see me? Well at least that's one less embarrassment to deal with" she remarked sarcastically.

As they were recalling the awkward spectacle, Sasha King breezed in behind the bar to start her shift. She smiled, a little uneasily, at the couple.

"Sasha…" started Lisa.

But Sasha immediately interjected, leaning over the counter

and apologising profusely. "I'm so sorry for speaking to Conor about your husband like that … I just felt it was important that he knew. You both looked so happy. I should have talked to you first Lisa. I'm Sorry"

A customer loudly beckoned at the far end of the bar. She turned, with an apologetic smile and headed off quickly to serve him. Lisa was puzzled and looked to Conor for an explanation.

He sighed. "Your husband came to Dover" he began.

"What?" Lisa exclaimed, shocked. "Ben was here?"

"Yeah… apparently he was coming to suss you out. He was sat here in the bar the same day that you and I came in here to get …well…plastered… the evening you told me all about Sharon.…"

"Oh my God… But we never even saw him…" Lisa threw her mind back to that evening. The only person she could think of was that man who had sat for the best part of an hour with his back to them at the end of the bar… the man drinking Guinness. Surely she would have recognised him… wouldn't she? Was she that preoccupied?

"Well anyway" Conor continued, "…after a couple of pints, he told Sasha who he was and why he was here…"

"Which was.…" probed Lisa impatiently.

"Which was to talk some sense into you I think… I reckon he was trying to get you to come home…but didn't know where to find you. Then, according to Sasha, when you came in, Sasha told him we were seeing each other and after about an hour of watching us together, he just got up and left… all he said to her was that 'you deserved to be happy'. Sasha told me everything the next day when I called in for lunch. Look, she felt awful for telling him about us, but she said that we both needed to know the gesture he had made, by just walking away. I would have told you sooner but with everything going on…"

Lisa nodded, a look of surprise and faraway sadness on her face.

"So Ben had a sensitive side after all? Pity he never showed it when we were together" she mused aloud.

Conor averted her distant gaze, looked to his pint and took a sip. Lisa smiled at him, realising his discomfort.

"...But I'm glad he never showed it", she said gently... "Otherwise I mightn't have left... and wouldn't have met you", she offered.

"Perish the thought", said Conor mockingly.

At that moment, they were interrupted by Lisa's phone ringing in her handbag. She rooted around and pulled it out. Conor continued to sip at his pint of Guinness, a creamy residue settling on his upper lip. Lisa wiped it off with a smirk as she answered the phone.

"Inspector?" she said anxiously.

Moments later, she had put down the phone, was beaming broadly and smugly lifting up her glass in front of her. "Inspector White has been in touch with the French authorities; they are already looking for Sharon and Bryan... and a Constabulary from the Kent Police are on their way to Calais as we speak... he hasn't so much as questioned my involvement, but I will have to make a statement as soon as they've been detained"

"Excellent" replied Conor. "Its over then... you can get on with your new life... here in Dover" he moved closer "... here with me" he whispered.

"Yes but..." she put the glass down again, before Conor had a chance to toast with her.

"But what?" he asked, his glass lingering in front of him.

"I just feel a little weird setting the police on them... Sharon and I had gotten kind of close. I mean... I really thought we were... friends"

Conor put his arm around her shoulders. "Lisa... it was all a lie. From beginning to end... your entire friendship was based on deceit

– putting you through a living hell so that she could get you where she wanted you. She told you a secret that she never meant you to keep… You did the right thing. I just hope she doesn't bring your name into it"

"She won't" Lisa said quietly - confidently.

"How can you be so sure?" Conor asked apprehensively.

Just then, before she could reply, the pub door opened again and in walked Riana. She was glowing with excitement. Lisa smiled awkwardly at her; shame bringing a rosy tinge to her cheeks. Riana smiled back. "Lisa don't even begin to apologise" she started "…it was an understandable mistake to make. I mean… he did have his arms wrapped around me… I would have thought the same thing…"

"Thanks Riana…for continuing to put up with my stupidity" said Lisa. "Where's your fiancé?"

"Oh he's just behind me…should be here in a sec… " As she spoke, the door opened again.

"Ah here he is…" began Riana proudly. "Lisa, I'd like you to meet my fiancé – Damien"

Lisa looked up; she suddenly began choking on the port she had just brought to her lips… after a moment of frantic coughing, she apologised. "Sorry" she began "Its just bloody hot" she said, hastily blaming the port and placing the glass back on the counter.

"Lisa" said Damien, who was as shocked and embarrassed to see Lisa, as she was to see him. "Eh … you ok?" he asked, concerned.

She nodded, truly mortified, as images of their many steamy encounters rushed through her mind.

Riana looked from one to the other.

"Do you guys know each other?" she enquired.

"…. No…" Damien started, embarrassed "…but think I may know your husband. Benjamin Gray isn't it?".

Lisa grinned. "That's right. Well, its nice to meet you", Lisa offered, holding her had out to Damien. He shook her hand, appreciating her subtlety and tact and smiled gratefully at her.

"Well" started Conor as he turned to face Lisa. "After all the drama over the past couple of days, do you think you will be staying in Dover for a bit longer?"

Lisa smiled. "Hmm, …I think I just might".

Riana sighed. "Of course she will! Now Lisa, you have to fill us in on all this 'drama'"

"Well" began Lisa… "It's a long story", she said, guiltily considering how she had been so quick to point the finger at Riana up until now "But I will definitely be very careful about who I choose to live next door to in the future"

"And no more keeping secrets" warned Conor playfully.

Riana nodded in light-hearted agreement. "Secrets can consume you in the end you know" she added teasingly.

"Oh I don't know", laughed Lisa, while winking discreetly at Damien

"…We all have our little secrets".

The End